death of the wolf

DODSFELL
BOOK TWO

MAVE HATHAWAY

Cover Design by Jess at Brushtoblades

Map Art by Mave Hathaway

Interior Art by Jess at Brushtoblades

Initial Edits: Ash & AL Splitleafsaturdays

Final Edits: Pages of Cedar

Formatting: Lofty Wings Press LLC

Paperback ISBN: 979-8-9907814-6-7

EBook ISBN: 979-8-9907814-7-4

Published by Lofty Wings Press LLC

Trust sneaks up on us all.
Suddenly you find yourself believing the person you spend the most time with. Never second guessing because they could never betray you.
This book is dedicated to those still stuck in the cycle. You can break it. I believe in you.

books by mave

BAELIAN EMPIRE

THE DODSTELL CHAPTER

The Breaking

Death of the Wolf

United We Fall coming in 2026

...more coming soon...

DRAGON LEGACY

The Apprentice

Training Camp

Ozzi Book 3 coming soon

...more coming soon...

trigger warning

- Death of a wife/parent
- Death during Childbirth
- Violence
- Torture
- Death
- Vague references to Suicide Ideation (No suicide happens or is recalled)

The Baelian Empire
Balthor
Dulvak
Dodsfell
Pahon
Temple
Drakore
Longspire
Meltem
Fae

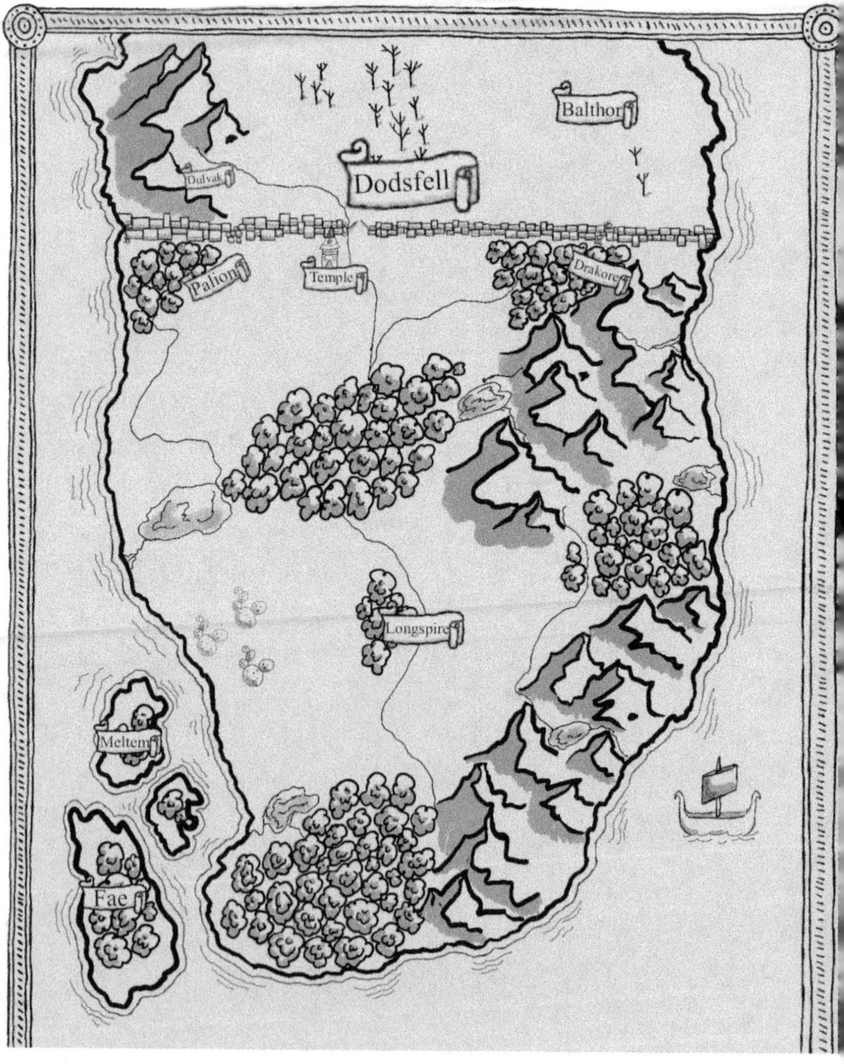

A Slice of Palion
The Wall
Palace Hill
Tiva Temple
Lykos Pub
Slums

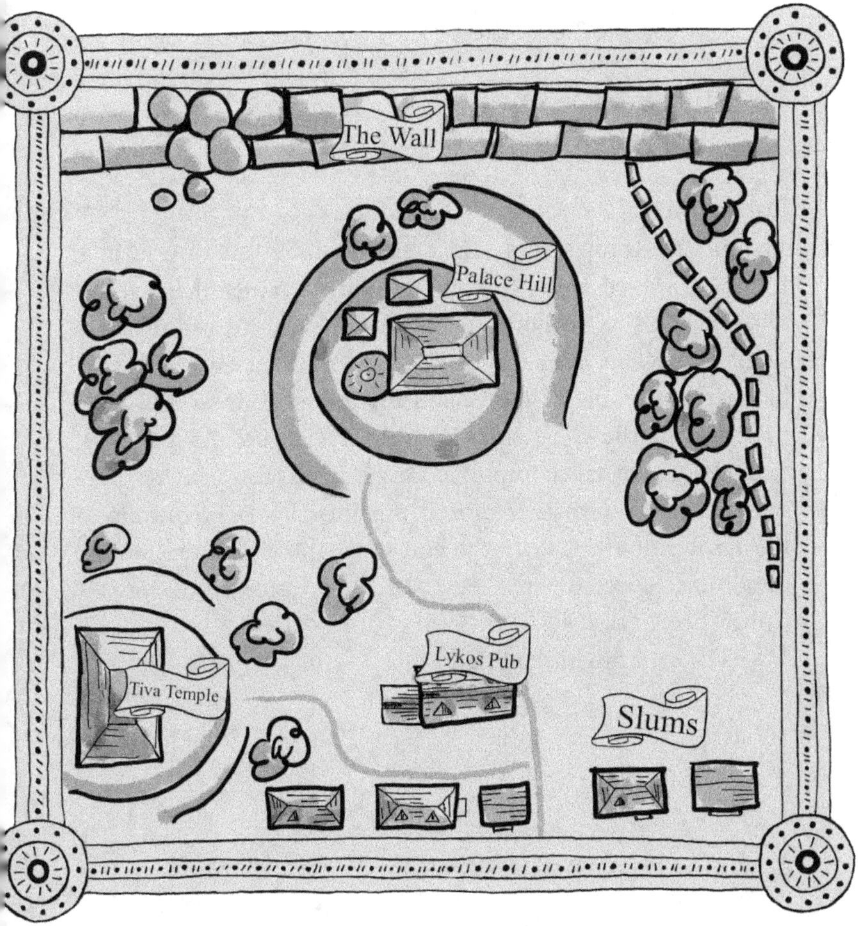

book blurb

Darling Mortal Readers,

Lucian Ronnet is the heir apparent to the throne in Palion. Destined to be brought up with a father that hates him, he looks to be alone. Yet I, the benevolent Lord of the Dead, have sent him a friend. It doesn't appear that my brother Lord Culgan appreciates my thoughtfulness, but all that does is show his small mindedness, right? As Lucian struggles to be taken more seriously, he is also striving to succeed in various other mortal pursuits. Love. Friendship. Boring if you ask me. By the end can I show him the most important aspect to life. Trust. After all, aside from yours truly, who can actually be trusted?

~Tixdarr Lord of the Dead

the enigma of time

Time is a tricky element in any civilization. Mortals live and die by a very strict calendar that for the Gods becomes rather flexible. As you read this book it is important to know that the timeline of Lucian's story runs parallel to the timeline of Aurelia's story found in *The Breaking*. I would like it noted that I have included a calendar for those mortals who may struggle keeping things in line. I do have limits to my patience however and have not added in every single festival that may be celebrated within Baelia. Be glad I decided to help at all.

~Tixdarr Lord of the Dead

Drak - Festival of Dragons *(Secretly Celebrated)*

Bura - Festival of New Life

Tiv - Festival of the Mother

Anit - Festival of Water

Byr - Festival of Fire

Duele - Festival of Harvest

Osi - Festival of Protection

Riari - Festival of Healing

Bene - Festival of Wind

Xita - Festival of War

Oxi - Festival of the Father

Tix - Festival of Death

religion hierarchy

It's important moving forward, wayward mortal, that you have a full idea of how our Pantheon functions. The Gods within the Pantheon each get a temple, but only if the people of the land choose to honor them with one. In the Kingdom you are about to visit they worship most frequently my brother Lord Culgan. He birthed the wolves and his temple there is rather intricate, though I still believe my temple is the best. I would of course hate for you to be confused so be sure to remember that the larger Gods have multiple small temples and one central one. Be advised moving forward in our universe, this is not an exhaustive list of Gods worshipped in Baelia. That would take far too much of my precious time.

~Tixdarr Lord of the Dead

TEMPLE POSITIONS:

- **Oba:** The head of the temple. One main Oba covers many smaller temples, only the strongest of the Gods warrant multiple Obas. This position has only ever been held by a woman, chosen by the God in question.
- **Abbot/Abbess:** The right hand to the Oba in the temple she resides in. In smaller temples this individual will run the temple and report issues to the God's chosen Oba.
- **Acolyte:** A member of the Gods order. Serves the temple and spreads the word of the God they all worship.

THE PANTHEON OF BAELIA

- **Goddess of Tiva** ~ Fairy ~ Goddess of Motherhood and Females
- **God Oxius** ~ Minotaur ~ God of Fatherhood and Males
- **God Tixdarr** ~ Demon ~ God of the Dead and Afterlife
- **God Burasil** ~ unknown species ~ God of Animal and Hunt
- **God Benmes** ~ Winged ~ God of Air and Wind
- **Goddess Deulla** ~ Centaur ~ Goddess of the Earth and Harvest
- **Goddess Byra** ~ Dwarf ~ Goddess of Fire
- **Goddess Anita** ~ Merfolk ~ Goddess of Water
- **God Xitar** ~ unknown ~ God of Fighting and War

- **God Osin** ~ unknown ~ God of Protection
- **Goddess Riarin** ~ Elf ~ Goddess of Healing and Medical
- **God Culgan** ~ Wolf ~ God of the Wolves

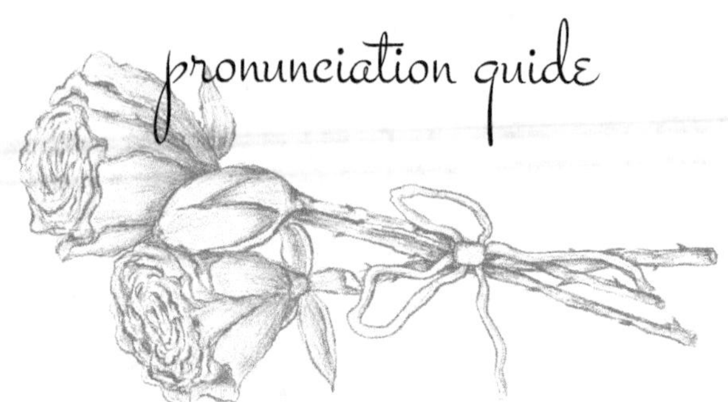

pronunciation guide

The other Gods have suggested that you may want to know how to pronounce the various names of things presented in this story. So here you go mortals parse through these words and figure out how to enter my world completely. ~Tixdarr Lord of the Dead

PEOPLE:

- Larial - (Lair-ee-al)
- Harold - (Hair-old)
- Naya - (Nye-uh)
- Vig - (V-ig)
- Suzu - (Sue-zoo)
- Zadon - (Z-aid-on)
- Lucian - (Loo-shin)
- Lykos - (Lai-kos)
- Ulfur - (Ul-ffur)
- Juro - (Jur-o)
- Marug - (Marr-ug)

- Sarina - (Sa-ree-na)
- Belvina - (Bell-vee-na)
- Dulvak - (Dull-va-k)
- Kana - (Kaw-na)

PLACE:

- Baelia - (Bay-lee-a)
- Palion - (Pal-ee-on)
- Drakore – (Drr-a-k-ore)

GODS:

- Goddess of Tiva - (T-ee-va)
- God Oxius - (Ox-ee-us)
- God Tixdarr - (Tick-star)
- God Burasil - (Brr-a-sil)
- God Benmes - (Ben-mis)
- Goddess Deulla - (Do-el-a)
- Goddess Byra - (Bi-ra)
- Goddess Anita - (A-ni-ta)
- God Xitar - (Zi-tar)
- God Osin - (Aw-sin)
- Goddess Riarin - (Ree-are-in)
- God Culgan - (K-ul-g-an)

MONTHS:

- Drak - (Dr-æ-k)
- Bura - (Brr-a)
- Tiv - (T-i-v)
- Anit (Æ-nit)

- Byr - (Bi-r)
- Duele - (Do-el)
- Osi - (O-see)
- Riari - (Ree-are-ee)
- Bene (Ben-a)
- Xita - (Zit-a)
- Oxi - (Ox)
- Tix - (Ticks)

prologue

HAROLD

PALION - BYR - YEAR 7539

> Palion and Drakore were both saddled with the task of protecting Baelia from the demons of Dodsfell. The Gods of the Pantheon ensued that the demons were locked away by Tixdarr, however it wasn't unheard of for an occasional demon to be released by the tricky God. Once the Gods had been locked away in the Void however both Palion and Drakore were left rather adrift. Demons became more of an anomaly to be assessed on a case by case basis and less of an enemy.
>
> ~Palion Archives

Harold gazed lovingly out the windows of his study. From this vantage point he could make out his gorgeous wife Larial strolling through the rolling fields of roses rubbing absently at her swollen belly. Warmth rolled through him at the sight of her maid. Finally she had conceded to reason. She was far too pregnant to carry anything even if it was only cut roses. She had a very unique process for picking out which ones were appropriate, looking at the smell, the color, and the size. All of which had to be perfect to grace the halls of their palace.

Roses were her very favorite flower. Once she had joined him in the palace to start their lives together, he had surprised her by planting them in every spare corner of the gardens, choosing varieties that would bloom no matter the season. He would give anything for her smile. He hadn't had a clue that planting so many would come in handy when she finally got pregnant. Now in the advanced stages, her sense of smell was exponentially intense. He teased her relentlessly about it being due to her wolf shifter genes.

In reality it truly amazed him at how clear she could smell despite the constant cloying aroma of roses. He couldn't even surprise her with her favorite desserts any longer because she could sniff out the chocolate in the air before he rounded the corner. He watched as Larial stroked a few roses, chatting animatedly with the maid. Soon she would be far too large to continue her walks around the gardens. His mind raced with ways he could bring the roses to her without killing them. A delicate balance to surprise without triggering the volatile pregnancy tears.

Their soulbonding was a unique one for many reasons. They were an interspecies pairing, Harold himself was from a tiger line of shifters while Larial was a gorgeous wolf shifter. Their meeting had felt like lightning had struck him in the heart, shocking and once in a lifetime. Yet, it wasn't without risk. The creation of children was complex. Interspecies matings weren't common. The Gods had as anyone could tell, not weighed in on the subject, but biology had. Most often the pregnancies of these matings resulted in disaster, if they were ever successful. Now that Larial was firmly pregnant, no one could clearly explain how the pregnancy would work. Instead they were left relying on the med witches to guarantee that she was safe throughout.

As most shifters did, Harold and Larial lived their life in their mortal shells, keeping the shifter forms for more special occasions. Mortals had a gestation of nine months, wolves a little over a month, while tigers gestated for around four months. It stressed him out that there were no guides in what to expect when you combined the three. They merely had to trust and hope the Gods blessed them with a safe delivery.

She had made it seven months, leaning into the idea that because they got pregnant while in their mortal shells she was following the mortal timeline. Yet if they were honest both of them expected she would deliver at any moment. All Harold cared about was that Larial came out of it on the other side healthy and happy. They had only been together for five years and he selfishly needed hundreds more.

He glanced at the sun and smiled. She would be making her way in for her midday snack any minute and he knew exactly where he wanted to be. The Kingdom could survive a few more hours of his distraction.

As he entered the cozy parlor she had outfitted to be her pregnancy den his heart rate doubled. She was bent over breathing deeply. No, not breathing, panting.

"Larial?" He couldn't halt the spike in his voice.

"Oh, hello dear." She panted a few more times while staring at the floor as if counting the fibers in the rug. "How's your day going darling?"

"No, no, what is happening with you?" He gestured to her bent nature, her hands unable to keep from clenching in pain.

"I...I think that the baby is headed this way." She squinted up at him, her green eyes clouded with pain. "I don't know for sure though. Naya said that there could be false labor."

Harold blinked his mind processing the words, a bit slower

than normal, fear freezing his blood. "Darling. This can't be false. Where are you set up for the delivery?"

He ran to the door and hollered out, "Someone get Naya NOW."

He returned to Larial and carefully put an arm around her shoulders. She laughed a bit. "Now, now Harold." She gasped clutching her middle taking the deepest inhale he'd ever witnessed. "All is fine. Just help me up to the guest room. Just think love, in a few hours we will have a little bundle of joy."

He nodded, doing his best to smile along with her. He couldn't keep the fear from clouding everything. He had a sense of foreboding that something would go deeply wrong. The trail of blood and liquid they were dripping as they ascended the marble staircase did nothing to assuage his mind.

Naya was in the room warming water and towels by the time they limped up there. She smiled warmly at him and took Larial by the shoulders. "Now Highness. I shall take her and see her through this part. Never fear. I will have my assistant come and update you when things are more progressed."

Harold glanced around and noticed a small wisp of woman in the corner pulling back the curtains flooding the room with light. He glanced back at his wife, his queen. "I could help..."

Larial turned and shot him a distracted smile. "No love, this part is said to be messy and could go on for a long while. I don't want to keep you from your duties. Go calm yourself with a drink. I'll see you in a bit."

Harold stood stupidly, his mouth agape. Uncertainty filled his every cell but he had little to argue with. He was not an expert in women's matters. Reluctantly he walked toward the door sending one more look back at his gorgeous wife. She stood bent over the bed in the center of the room, Naya and her assistant aiding in stripping her out of her formal gowns. He stepped into the hall just as a wail ripped from her throat.

His blood turned to ice. He should be in there holding her hand. He should help. Yet, she herself told him no.

He paced in front of the door shaking off any servant who tried to pull him from his vigil. Every time her voice rose in distress his blood spiked. Heat filled his hands and he had to stomp on the base urge to strangle anyone who hurt her. His magic over growing things had long since been mastered but with his mind in such turmoil it wasn't listening, vines beginning to crawl haphazardly up the walls. He began to chant quietly to himself with every step, he paced up and down the hall. *This was their child. This was normal. This was fine. That's what society claimed after all.*

After around ten distressing calls echoing through the closed door Harold was done with being patient. "Enough is enough."

He shoved the door open, and the assistant squeaked in dismay. Naya had only enough spare energy to glance at him and roll her eyes. "If you're going to be a caveman, go by her head and hold her hand. Honestly, men think they can do everything."

His eyes were on his wife's face. Pale. Sweat streaked. Creased with pain. His heart stuttered. "Lar?"

She merely had a second to look at him before her entire abdomen shuddered and a scream of pain shredded her throat. He ran to her all propriety of his kingly title forgotten. "Lar. It's going to be fine. Just breathe."

He reached around her shoulders, bracing, taking more of her weight, aiding in keeping her sitting up. She met his eyes as he pushed her sweat streaked hair off her face. Her head was burning up. Panic filled him.

He looked down at Naya and as if she could read his mind she shook her head. "Don't start questioning me. We are doing what we can. I already know."

Harold swallowed his words instead refocusing on his

beloved. Quickly he shed his boots and overcoat. The belt and sheath were next landing next to the bed in a heap. Then he unceremoniously climbed up behind her. Cradling her body between his legs, his chest supporting her back. "Use me. Push against me next time, love. I can take it. Let me help."

She had no strength to talk, just nodded once. Another ripple occurred across her stomach and her hands gripped into his thighs. He chanted. "Breathe love. Breathe. You're doing so good my love. Just a few more seconds. You got this." As the ripple ended, he glanced at Naya, and she nodded at him. He felt better knowing what he was doing was potentially helping her.

The sun was setting, and they hadn't made any noticeable movements toward a delivery. Naya and her assistant were standing to the side, whispering in hushed tones. Larial had fallen into a slumber on him. But he couldn't settle. Larial's skin had continued to pale, the skin beneath her eyes looked darker, her lips stained blue around the edges. Something was wrong and they weren't telling him. He couldn't fix it if they didn't tell him. He had this immense power connected to Baelia itself, yet they wouldn't tell him.

"Naya." He said it harshly but tried not to yell. Larial didn't even twitch. Her breathing even and unbothered. Naya turned and came reluctantly toward them. "What is happening?"

She glanced at her Queen and then muttered quickly and so quietly he almost missed it. "The babe appears to be coming out the wrong way. It should emerge headfirst and flow through the canal but with every push I only feel feet. It's possible the babe will perish if we can't get it out."

Harold nodded his mind mulling over the idea. "What happens to her if it does?"

Naya looked down and muttered. "Either way sire the

babe must come out. To do that we have to cut her, which would be disastrous."

Harold blinked. Larial wasn't connected to the Great Land Power due to how they were married. She couldn't heal like he could. A large incision would end with her death. "You are telling me my mate is dying?"

Naya nodded, a tear escaping. "I don't know how to fix this, Highness. It's a truly rare complication."

He nodded but Larial's voice now raspy from her earlier screaming spoke before he could. "If I am to die you will save my child. Naya, do you understand?"

Naya glanced at him and then back to the blinking Larial. "Yes, Your Majesty. I shall prepare the instruments."

"Harold. It's important that you listen to me. I need you to care for this child. To love it like I would if I was given a chance to." She smiled, her face finally relaxing. "You know we never talked about names. I want Enora for a girl or Lucian for a boy."

Harold's throat felt blocked due to emotions. Yet he pushed past and spoke. "Why those my love?"

"They mean light and you my darling Harold have been the light in my life. I want this child to be yours."

Harold nodded, kissing the top of her head. His mind stuttering over her acceptance of her death. "Lar. I can't lose you. I shall come with you. The child can be raised by your family in the wolf clan. Don't leave me."

She reached up to his face, her body moving slow, "No. Harold, you need to promise me you will raise our child. That is your priority now. Naya?" Her voice raised to a demand.

Naya rushed over, "Yes, Your Majesty."

"I need a dagger. Quick now before you get started."

Naya didn't even blink at the request, merely pulled one from a deep pocket in her skirt. Larial smiled and nodded her thanks. Without hesitation she sliced deep into her palm and turned the knife into his thigh. The only skin of his readily available. He grunted as she slapped her cut hand against his leg, preventing the Great Power from immediately sealing it.

"I, Larial Ronnet, charge you Harold Ronnet with the responsibility to live your life and raise our child despite my loss. You must push past the pain."

Harold's lip trembled, tears leaking out of his eyes as he nodded. "I, Harold Ronnet, accept your terms and vow to you Larial, love of my life, that I shall push past the pain."

The magic of the oath flowed through them and Naya brought a tray of tools. "Once I start it won't take long. I am so sorry there is no other way, mistress."

Larial gave a watery smile. "Fret not. I do not blame you my dear."

She gripped Harold tightly. He swallowed past his pain and pulled her chin toward him. "One more for luck." He fastened his mouth on hers wanting nothing more than to drown in her taste, unwilling to part with the best thing to ever have happened to him.

Finally Larial broke the kiss, tears in her eyes a smile on her face. Her hand drifted up between them tucking some hair behind his ear. "I'll love you forever, Harold."

She turned and nodded to Naya. Naya hadn't been lying, it only took a few minutes of slicing, each swipe causing more blood to drench the bed and floor. Larial screaming more and more and then before he knew what was happening the screams of a baby joined her.

Naya threw a blanket over Larial's abdomen and swaddled the newborn. She brought it up swiftly to Larial's face. "Mistress. Focus, focus here. Here is your son."

Larial smiled weakly, her arms not quite up to gripping. Harold aided her in bringing them up and aided her in cradling the screaming boy. "Lucian."

Harold blinked. He had a son. But he was losing his wife.

He watched as her eyes flickered. Closing then opening even slower.

Harold took control over the situation. "Naya, take the baby." She moved quickly, tears pouring from her. "Larial please look at me one more time." Her green gaze fixed on him, a smile on her face.

"Harold, I love you so much more than you will ever realize. I shall wait for you on the other side my darling." Her eyes stayed on his but took on a glazed look that spoke to the absence of a soul. Her chest rose one last time before it stilled. Harold held his breath aiming only to breath out when she did, but soon his own lungs burned.

He gasped for air, crying out. "My love, you are the reason for me existing. I was made for you. I don't know how I will go on. I love you so much. Love. Love?"

A roar of pain emerged as the assistant came over gently closing Larial's eyes for the last time. His soul ripped from his body leaving naught but a scrap behind. Naya cuddled the baby rocking him in tempo to her own sobs, turning away from the now dead Queen.

"Take the baby to a nursemaid." At Naya's hesitation Harold growled, "I know my oath, woman. Yet it was highly specific. I will raise him, and I will live despite the overwhelming desire I have to join her in the Void." He closed his eyes tightening his hold on her cooling body. "I can't. I can't look at the cause of her demise. If I do, I may kill him myself. It's safer for him away from me."

Harold curled around his wife hoping to hold on to her soul for just a few more minutes. Yet, her body was already beginning to lose its vivacious heat, dulling towards the coolness that represented death.

He sobbed until he could no longer function. As the tears dried his body grew stiff and pained. The oath mark on his thigh throbbed, a painful reminder that he was beholden to her even in her death. He took a deep breath inhaling her unique scent one more time his brain rearranging itself as he tried to come to terms with his new reality. He pulled himself up, resolutely turning from the body that had once held his true love. He stepped into the hall to find Kana the Oba of Tixdarr waiting with acolytes to collect her body.

"My condolences, sire. Also my congratulations on the birth of your heir. At least she fulfilled her duty before the Gods recalled her."

A darkness foreign and yet comforting at the same time flared within him as he snarled. "If you want that damn temple guarded and cared for, you will shut your mouth. Get on with what you are here for. My steward will arrange the Rite as is proper."

Kana nodded once, entering the room where he had left his only shred of kindness. Larial had been his grounding force. Between the Gods and Lucian, they now held the responsibility for what he was left with. Lucian would always hold the blame because he had taken his mother's life.

ONE

HAROLD

PALION - BYR - 7554

Harold stood in the shadows of his office, watching his son and his son's new friend, wander through the rose gardens. The way Lucian carried himself was so reminiscent of Larial that it caused his heart to stop when he wasn't paying attention and only caught glimpses of his profile in the distance.

As the boy grew, Harold had tried to grow some level of affection for him. He stood on the sidelines watching all the children in the court, and oftentimes found a few of them as entertaining or affectionate, yet when he would observe his own child he just felt intense levels of disdain. An attempt at affection quickly shifted to attempting to tolerate and prep the boy for his eventual succession to the throne. It just never stuck, tolerating him seemed to add levels of hate on top of the disdain that had festered in his childhood.

The reasons for his negativity in regards to his only child

always came back to one specific issue. When he dared to look the boy in the face he couldn't see Lucian, instead he saw her. Larial's dying face echoed back to him through the eyes of her son. Then his mind would betray him replaying the blood smeared sheets, hearing her cries of pain. As Lucian grew the idea of replacing him occurred. He could find a likely lad in the village, train the newcomer to rule once Harold grew too old to continue. He had even begun taking interviews with boys around the same age, fifteen. His first candidate was set to appear in his office in another hour or so.

A loud stomping sounded outside his office, before he knew what was happening the door was thrown open with no preamble. He turned slowly toward the intruder a glare ready as he laid eyes on Naya, Lucian's nanny turned governess. "What are you doing, Harold?!"

Harold raised an eyebrow. "I don't believe I gave you permission to refer to me in such informal ways. However, I am currently observing *my* kingdom. Do pray tell, explain what you are doing."

She glowered her chest heaving with emotion, "You are holding interviews for a new son? How dare you! Lucian will hear of this through gossip in the palace. You can't seriously think he would stay ignorant. What would Larial say?"

Anger raced into his veins at the disrespect along with the audacity that she had to bring his beloved into the fight. "I am holding interviews for an heir. In no way will they be my son, they will merely be my apprentice. I dare because I CAN. I am the King but you seem to have forgotten that reality. I could care less if Lucian knows as it will be abundantly apparent when he doesn't get the Great Power of the Land. He is destined for nothing. Larial isn't here to have an opinion. You are lucky to still be here after taking it upon yourself to teach him about times that will never happen again."

She looked at him, the glare still holding strong. "He

deserves to know that at one point there was love between you two. He deserves to know he was wanted by at least one of you!"

Harold strode over to his desk. "You are not the instructor, you have not been given permission to teach him that. Nor do you get to try and repair the bond you think is broken. Stay in your lane Naya or get out. Your position is only here because you were important to *her*. Since she is no longer here, you are at risk of being removed from our service, for your behavior."

Naya's face turned into a storm cloud. "It is a bond that you refused to form. She oath bonded you to raise your child, yet you just sit there and rule with a frigid fist without any semblance of empathy. You are not holding your end of the bargain and I am shocked by the Gods leniency."

"Gods are fickle things aren't they. They keep to the letter of the oath and guess what. I have ensured he lived. I paid you to keep him so, when he was too young to fend for himself. I hired tutors to teach him. I have just supplied him a friend when it became apparent he lacked the needed social skills. Never in my oath did I agree to love him, or free him from the appropriate levels of consequence to the death of his mother." Harold began to write out her dismissal notice his hand shaking with the emotion.

"She died due to an accident, HAROLD. Lucian didn't do anything to cause her death. You are avoiding dealing with your emotions and it needs to stop for your own health!" Naya growled.

"No. You are mistaken. He chose to come early. If he had stayed in longer then she would have survived." He held up her dismissal slip. "Your services are no longer needed. I expect you to leave the premises immediately. There will be no seeking out Lucian, you will simply disappear."

Her face paled leaving him satisfied. "You will regret this."

"Doubtful but time and the Gods will tell." He stood still

waiting for her to leave the room before he sank into his office chair. His mind pulled him under the weight of grief and memories, causing tears to fall unbidden on onto his jacket. All thoughts of replacing Lucian, the inept teenager, as his heir flooded away from his mind as the tears fell.

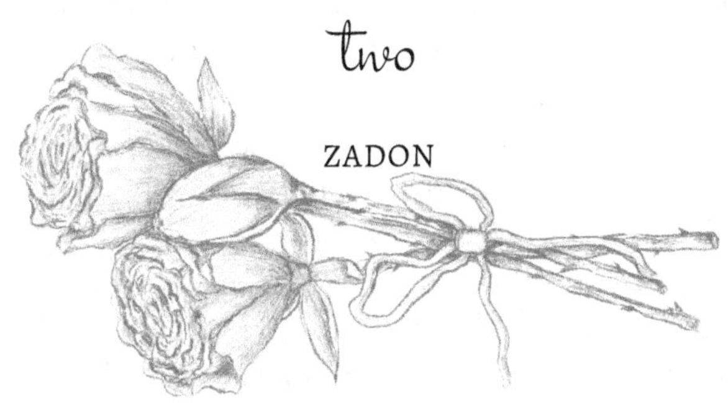

two

ZADON

All he could see in front of him were the heads and shoulders of mortal bodies all pushing and jostling against one another hoping to edge closer to the dias in the front. The marble walls of the elaborate ceremony chamber made the noise echo indefinitely, causing his ears to ring painfully. The tangy smell of unwashed mortal bodies left Zadon's mouth watering, his demonic nature craving to indulge in just a small taste. His usual coping mechanism of deep breaths wasn't working, made evident as a quick glance at his hands showed blue talons where once there had been mortal fingers.

His mind reeled fighting for control over his baser instincts. He turned his thoughts away from his current predicament, focusing instead on his reasons for being stuck in the hell hole of a mortal realm. It wasn't a large leap of logic, the current press of bodies reminiscent of the bodies that pushed him out of his home.

His own clan, the Duvlak, the ones who raised him,

trained him, and he had thought loved him. These were the creatures pulling and pushing at him shoving him through the magic. It had been one dark night three years prior, they had pulled him from his bed, shoving him toward the Great Gate, jeering and screeching their dissatisfaction. He knew Estrez, the Matriarch of the clan, had ordered his removal but that knowledge only opened up more questions. She had to have gone to get the banishment blessed by Tixdan. For the life of him he couldn't understand why. It was one of the greatest dishonors for a demon to be banished from Dodsfell and hadn't happened in centuries.

The journey to Palion had not been easy, he had expected to die once his feet landed in Baelia. After all his 'family' had beaten him close to death before shoving him through the magic. The pain had seared through his entire being, burning so hot he lost consciousness for a few minutes. His mortal shell had been feeble, spending two days buried in snow, naked, so bruised and broken he couldn't pull himself upright even if he had wanted to. Somehow, someone from the temple had come across him, given his situation they had to have had divine intervention but... Which God was responsible? He could only guess. A shout echoing through the chamber brought his consciousness back to the present. His glance at Lucian at the front of the room directed his memories to King Harold. Divine intervention had to have played a part into King Harold's role in Zadon's life. The King had ushered him into the Palace clearing the way for him to become Prince Lucian's closest friend. Three years holding that title had gone by in a blur, and it had become obvious in that time that the King had a misbegotten idea that Zadon's stern demon persona would rub off on Lucian. Perhaps with the intent of creating a hardened ruler, especially because there was such a deep rift between the ruler and his son.

Someone pushed him hard between the shoulder blades

jerking his mind back into the present. Reminding him that he needed to continue on his journey to get back home. He needed something that would open the damn gate once more. He forced a smile, which he had no doubt appeared grotesquely disfigured, as those around him shifted away, looks of fear on the faces of the women. He internally grumbled at having to keep his mask of a dutiful companion on, while biding his time for freedom.

He turned his attention back to the dias with sheer force of will, staring at the young man in the front of the room. Lucian, his medium build quivering with nerves, appeared pleased and shy at all the attention. Positivity in general was rather a foreign concept to the young man. The noise swelled as the cheering reached a crescendo. Large wolven mortals jostled around Zadon all excitedly watching the ceremony occurring. An Alpha ceremony only happened once every few hundred years with the length of time most shifters lived. This new ceremony would end with every wolf in the room being able to mind speak with the Prince of Palion. It was the first time in a very long time that an Alpha wolf had the possibility of being on the throne. From what Zadon had figured out it was more than likely due to the Queen's bloodline, though he hadn't been able to confirm that.

As the jostling increased the room felt ever smaller. The marble walls seeming to slowly enclose around him forcing the wolves to encroach on his personal space. Zadon took deep breaths forcing calm thoughts to run through his mind.

He stared ahead, a smile plastered on his face just in case anyone was watching him. His mask all that kept him alive, if anyone got a whiff that he hadn't set aside his demonic ways, they would neutralize the threat he posed to mortals. Unfortunately for him, a lone demon in a world made for the living, he would struggle. Demons were inherently a pack creature, thriving on each others strength to hunt and kill.

He glanced down at the table and saw Lucian's goblet, an idea surfacing through the pain. His demon side surged forward in his mind eager to react, eager to play, eager to toy with a person's life. His sense of self preservation fell to the side as he casually reached over, picking up the intricately decorated gold goblet by the brim. Zadon raised it as if toasting to Lucian's new role never altering his grip on the goblet. Under the cover of the chaos around, he let his pointer finger elongate into his demon talon, sharp, a glistening blue in the candle light. He took a second to stare at his talon, he missed his demon side. He hadn't worn his true skin in so long because it wasn't acceptable in the mortal realm. He rolled his shoulders releasing the feelings that welled within him.

Slyly without drawing much attention, he let his taloned finger slice across the wrist still hovering above the glistening wine. He shifted the goblet intent to ensure that all the blood drizzling out of him made it into the cup.

He let his blood drip until the cut healed itself. It was at most ten drops but given the potency of demon's blood it would be enough. His lips locked in a warm smile towards Lucian as he bowed at the elder Alpha before taking a knee. Zadon swirled the contents of the goblet, glancing down to ensure that it all mixed together. The only indication that something had been added to the wine was a slight sheen on the top of the liquid.

As casually as possible he placed the goblet down on the table. He began to clap as the Elder Alpha took Lucian's head in his hands and they touched foreheads, the initiation having begun in earnest. Lucian's body began to change, shifting into a large dark gray wolf with white spots periodically throughout his coat. Almost like stars in the sky. The Elder Alpha shifted into his own wolf, a wizened creature that appeared a bit sunken, as if the years weighed heavily on his head. The brown coat a bit duller than the shiny dark of

Lucian's coat. As this occurred the room that had seconds before been filled with cheers and hollering fell silent. Every single wolven shifter, closing their eyes becoming a part of the ceremony, entering a trance like state in order to join consciousness with Lucian. Ultimately, Zadon found shifter behaviors and quirks interesting, if every demon could contact their clan matriarch it would make hunting so much easier. His situation would never have come to pass and he may have even been able to continue living within Dodsfell.

three

LUCIAN

PALION - BENE - YEAR 7557

He had managed to get his father to allow them to use the official ceremony chamber in the northern tower of the palace for the ritual. It was easily the largest room at their disposal. It lent a feeling of prestige to the entire tradition which made it more dignified than the field where this formal event typically happened. He had the room decorated in Ronnet colors, white and yellow, hoping it would encourage his father to appear and show the crown's formal approval. The amount of cheering that filled the room grew louder as he took a knee in front of the Elder Alpha. It sent a thrill down his spine, while simultaneously scaring him. *Could this be taken away? Would his father allow this?* As the noise grew in crescendo it reached such heights that he worried it may bring the roof down around them.

His attention was brought back to the present as the Elder Alpha leaned over him. It was apparent that the ritual was taking its toll on the ancient man, his breathing heavy and in short bursts. It had been a surprise when the Alpha had come to the palace all those months ago, explaining how Culgan the God of the Wolves had sent a dream. He had extolled that within the dream he had seen Lucian Ronnet, taking charge and leading the wolves to great victories, able to bestow honor and light to all who were blessed to be a wolf shifter. Lucian had been in shock absolutely certain there had been a mistake, his father King Harold, had gone so far as to send for the Oracle and demand explanations. Yet despite the interspecies mating of his parents, or perhaps because of it the Gods saw him as a strong contender for the Alpha title.

As it became more obvious that this event had indeed been ordained by the Gods, Lucian began to hold a naive boy's hope. Hope that his father would finally see more than the flaws that continued to hold sway in his eyes. Yet despite the preparations and the various discussions with the Elder Alpha on Wolf politics, Lucian had only seen disgust and disbelief displayed by his father. His father's words filtered through his mind. *"You are a useless man child, incapable of even the simplest errands there's absolutely no way that the Gods would give you such an honor."*

He refocused his attention on the task at hand. The Elder Alpha gripped his head pulling so that their foreheads touched. Their breaths mingled for a few minutes, causing Lucian's mind to calm from the revulsion of his father. His skin stretched, the bones elongating within his body. It had once been painful, but he had shifted so much as a teen to escape his father that his wolf side was a safe place. There were a few pops and then he resided safely inside the skin of his wolf, happiness filling his mind. The Elder Alpha's wolf appeared where his mortal shell once was. Lucian felt a sadness fill him at the sight of the Elder's wolf. Shrunken, and tired the fur more gray than brown this close up, the shine dulled away by time.

The happiness of being home within his wolf faded as his mind filled with a buzzing. Almost as if a thousand bees had suddenly been released inside his skull and they were angry. The buzzing gradually morphed, into words. Words from a thousand different voices. Those of the old and young all joined together in a unique harmony within his mind. Filling his head to an extent that his skull felt like it was cracking under the pressure to keep all the personas inside.

If the Elder was mistaken about him being the heir this process would undoubtedly kill him, his brain exploding due to the amount of visitors pushing in. Fear spiked in his blood as the pressure continued to build, heat beginning to form behind his eyes and at the contact on his forehead. His instinct was to step away to pull his face away from the Elders, yet just as he lifted his back leg to step the pain began to subside. Going from a sharp fullness to more of a dull thump, an echo of what had been.

In the aftermath a thousand different voices remained in his head, speaking inside his mind. *How do I handle this?* Luckily it seemed that his own thoughts were not being projected to those within his mind. He would need to figure out how to project thoughts when needed to those of his pack. *His pack.* That had him stopping in the process of shifting, awe filling him. He had people now who looked to him first, that relied on him, that believed in him, not his father. It dawned on him that this was the first time in his life that anyone would see Lucian as the holder of power.

The Elder Alpha shifted and stood back smiling down encouragingly at Lucian knowing full well the struggle he was dealing with in his mind. Lucian hadn't believed the Elder Alpha when he tried to impart the teachings of how to handle the mental change. He thought the Elder had used it as a ploy to get Lucian to do his bidding. It wouldn't be the first time that someone in power had stretched a truth in order to manipulate Lucian into something. He finally shifted, leaving behind his wolf form and stepping into his Alpha role after bowing toward the Elder. Unable to contain his smile, he turned back toward the crowd bowing to them as he had been instructed.

He caught sight of Zadon standing, at one of the many tall tables strewn across the room. He was holding two elaborately decorated golden goblet's, a large welcoming smile on his face. Lucian returned the happy smile, a feeling of unmatched joy bubbling within him, that his best friend had gotten to be there and see him get this glorious honor. Doing his best to shove the various voices filtering through his mind to the side, he joyfully walked down the steps of the podium. The crowd parted for him, only a few reverently reaching out to graze his sleeve. He chose to ignore it, far too focused on the excitement. He neared the table where Zadon stood and grinned like a school boy. "Did you see Zadon!"

"Of course my brother, of course. You did great. How did the joining feel? It looked intense and everyone out here got so quiet. It was pretty interesting."

Lucian looked down remembering the oath he had sworn with the Elder, "I can't quite put my finger on it Z but it was a gift for sure. I won't forget that moment."

Zadon nodded and handed over a goblet. "I snagged you the finest wine, the kitchen servants have pulled it from deep within the cellars. It's a gift from your father I hear."

Lucian's ears pricked up at that surprised that his father would think to give him anything. "That is surprising. I hope it actually tastes good, have we had it tested for poison? He hasn't even given me a gift for a birthday my entire life."

His mind filled with images of lonely birthdays. Large birthday cakes with only his nursemaid turned governess Naya in attendance. No one ever came to parties despite her attempts to invite any children on the palace grounds. It took years to figure out why but when he turned fifteen it became obvious. After she sent out the invitations a royal decree would follow, making the palace do some sort of event scheduled on the day Naya set aside for his birthday party. That had all ended when Zadon had been thrust into his life, Naya dismissed by his father without a second thought.

Lucian's focus returned to the present as Zadon shrugged noncommittally and tipped back his own goblet taking a huge swallow. Wine dribbled out of his mouth as a predatory smile appeared, "I would have to say Lucian this is some of the finest wine I've ever tasted. Even back when we snuck into the cellars and opened a keg that first year I was here. I'll take it off your hands if you don't want it." Zadon stuck out his hand ready to snatch the goblet from Lucian's own fingertips.

Lucian laughed at him "No, no you can't take this." He tipped the goblet back and swallowed it down in two gulps, his throat opening up and accepting the liquid so quickly he barely tasted it.

four

ZADON

PALION - BENE - YEAR 7557

" The wolf shifting gene is an elusive one. So elusive that the successful transfer from generation to generation has begun to be tracked. There are times where families consisting of two wolf shifters give birth to a child that can barely sustain the wolf form, only having a modicum of access to the Great Power. It is whispered in the larger Palion pack that the gene is only passed on with the blessing of Lord Culgan, God of the Wolves. Should he turn up his nose at you, your child will be cursed.

~ Culgan Temple Archives

Zadon smiled broadly as Lucian's throat bobbled. It took mere seconds for the goblet to be drained, glee filling Zadon as he waited to see what effect, if any, would happen to the measly mortal. In the mortal realms it was unheard of for a demon to

"

force its blood down the throat of a living creature. Yet, in Dodsfell things were different. Infrequently the magical barrier separating the realms allowed a mortal in and the demons took their time torturing the poor soul until it lost its grip on reality. Part of that torture included feeding their blood to the mortals involved. It tended to result in the victim experiencing intense pain. There were rumors that sometimes there could be even more intense reactions.

Lucian put the goblet down triumphantly on the table. "You can't take my father's wine away." He paused, a look of confusion flitting across his face. "It tastes a little off though." Lucian patted his stomach a bit as if to see that the wine stayed where it had been put. Zadon held his breath expecting more, but nothing more came.

Zadon shrugged letting out the held breath on a sigh looking around, taking note that the ceremony seemed to be dissolving into a party. "What is the plan for this evening, my Prince?"

He glanced back at Lucian, his curiosity peaking as he took in Lucian's eyes glazing over.

"Sire?" Zadon dragged in a lungful of air, waiting. Lucian remained silent, staring off into the distance, his eyes unfocused. He walked around Lucian assessing, nothing looked physically different, given the new alphadom perhaps the issue was with his wolf duties but something didn't feel right.

Zadon touched Lucian's shoulder, gripping it and shaking slightly. "Lucian?" He leaned closer to the Prince's face, getting within a few inches. "Lucian, talk to me."

A voice that didn't sound like the Prince's normal one emerged, it was dark and husky. "What?" This voice sounded mean and jaded where Lucian typically sounded kind and understanding.

"Do you need the Elder Alpha? Has something gone wrong?"

"No."

Interesting. He expected to see a reaction. One where Lucian was screaming gripping his stomach in pain, however he remained stoic and calm if a bit stiff. Zadon's demonic side sagged a bit in disappointment within his mind. The goal of chaos and pain, indulging his hidden side, seemed to have failed. He gripped Lucian's shoulder a bit harder than necessary, steering the Prince toward the edge of the room angling for a bit of privacy. Once they reached a quiet corner Lucian's breathing had begun to come in short bursts, his face a mask of anger and violence. "What do you need, Lucian?"

"Blood. Pain. Kill."

"I see. Well. That's a problem we can fix." He scanned the room not willing to utilize this violence against a wolf given the current situation and the possible repercussions of an Alpha killing a member of the pack. He needed to get a better handle on the inner workings of the wolf pack dynamics before encouraging such actions. Then he saw it. A group of young panther shifters across the room beginning to cause their own version of mayhem. He leaned toward Lucian whispering for his ears alone. "Just keep a handle on whatever this is until we can get outside."

five

LUCIAN

PALION - BENE - YEAR 7557

As the liquid slid down his throat it settled heavy in his stomach making the food he had eaten earlier roll uneasily. His consciousness reeled with too many inputs; the wolf pack teeming on the edges of his mind demanding attention, and his soul having sensation for the first time in his memory. His soul or what he assumed was his soul, tingled to the point of pain. The stinging crested until he felt as if his inner self had become cleaved into two separate beings. The heavy liquid oozed within him, greasy oil, attaching to his soul.

Another pain began in his body, a stabbing within his gut. His instinct was to double over, but he tried his best to remain passive. He wouldn't be the reason that this opportunity of reliance would be ruined. If the pack realized what was happening, perhaps they would rescind the Alpha title. He had to be strong.

His consciousness became swamped suddenly with a heavy darkness that weighed upon his mind. His body bowed with the pressure. He couldn't think. He couldn't process what was happening. His vision seemed to be gone. He could hear Zadon speaking but couldn't figure out how to use his own voice to answer. After an internal struggle a darker, sinister voice came from his own throat shocking him.

Lucian attempted to speak but it only came out within his mind, "*What is happening to me?*"

A darker voice answered him echoing within his own mind, different from the voices of the wolves, this one tinged in oil. "*You are mine now boy. My vessel. I shall use you to further my aims.*"

Lucian's soul balked at this implied threat. Not understanding what it could mean, or what was possible. A need surged within him, foreign and frightening. A need to do violence to feel another being writhe in pain. He didn't know what to do about it. He had never been one for brutality. His father had chosen to administer violence on him any chance that presented itself. He had sworn he would be a different man, that when it was his time as ruler there would be a change.

His mind reeled as the feeling of passion swelled, passion towards cruelty. Lucian rebelled as hard as he could. He didn't understand where this new feeling came from, but his mind screamed into the void. He could feel his wolf try to take control, his body trying to shift, but this foreign oily substance was preventing it. It also created a wall within his mind snuffing out the sounds of the pack.

Lucian's vision was still compromised the only indication that Zadon led him around was the hand on his upper bicep. From the scent, he had led them towards the back gardens. Rose clinging to everything. Some of the whispered assurances filtered through the darkness, "All is well Sire. Stay calm just a few more minutes."

Yet the need to inflict pain was drowning out even Zadon's

voice. The dark and sinister voice chanting *beat, cut, bleed, pain give me pain.* Zadon disappeared leaving Lucian swaying, unsteady on his feet as the malevolence grew louder. He began to pace, or try to, it was more like a staggered shuffle to bleed off the excess energy. Yet all it did was get stronger. New sounds began to filter into his mind, jokes and silliness of young people. A deep inhale brought the smell of panther into his nostrils. Stoking a flame within his newfound immorality. He stepped into the shadow of the castle, the panther shifters unaware of any danger that could be lurking around.

A male came into view first and still Lucian waited. Once the second figure emerged past the wall, he pounced. Leaping onto the male his arm snaked around the neck of his victim. His superior size and the element of surprise allowed him to neutralize the threat swiftly. He quickly turned, the crunch of gravel betraying the presence of a third panther. It was Lucian's turn to scream as talons tore through his fingers morphing his hand. Unable to stop to consider what was happening, or where his wolf claws had gone, he used the newfound talons to stab through the chest of the third panther. He grasped the still beating heart as the panther shifter managed no more than a strangled squawk before Lucian pulled the heart steaming into the night air. The evil inside growled in satisfaction. At this point the first male had turned toward the fight his mouth hanging open a goblet still clutched in his hand. The goblet landed on the ground at the same time that Lucian landed on the man. A squeal of distress was all that could emerge before Lucian ripped his throat out.

The fight didn't last long. His newfound strength whether from the inky shadows that were dwelling within or the Alpha ceremony, gave him the ability to tear the men limb from limb. The fight began to blur around him Lucian starting to only see the red mist that flew. Zadon stepped up to him before

Lucian even realized that the fight was over and took him by the shoulder.

"Let us head this way my friend." Lucian could barely make out the servants corridor that Zadon led them up. As the door of his own chambers closed the darkness finally retreated. Zadon began to flick off the worst of the gore from Lucian's body.

"What is going on Zadon?" He whispered the question unsure he even wanted the answer.

"It's yet to be seen Lucian. I don't know for sure."

He couldn't get his arms to work, unable to remove the blood drenched clothes. Zadon noticed his struggle and strode over carefully peeling off the clothes. Lucian's teeth chattered as a breeze wound its way through the bathing chamber cooling his wet skin. Zadon continued to aid him, sluicing water over him with a cup. It took longer than normal to get clean. It was as if the loss of the blood coating his skin freed the last of the shadows from his immediate mind. His body began to move under his own direction.

He took the proffered towel from Zadon, draping it around his waist as he limped toward the wardrobe. Flashes of what had just occurred floated through his mind. *Did that really happen? Perhaps this is some massive misunderstanding.* He picked out the softest clothing he could, changing before he began to pace, limp and all, attempting to understand what had just occurred. It felt like a hundred years had passed aging his mind, while flashes of red mist floated across his vision. The joy of the wolf ceremony long forgotten.

Zadon threw himself into a velveted chair in his living area, toweling off the bits of gore that had splashed him. "Do you still feel the wolves within you?"

Lucian opened his mouth to answer but hesitated. "I can but the connection seems farther away. The wolves are quieter than before."

Zadon nodded, "Perhaps that's normal."

"I don't think so. I was told they would basically be all I think about, other work and responsibilities would take extra effort to focus my attention. Will you... will you clean up the bodies?"

Zadon nodded his face the same neutral it had been the entire time. "Yes, yes. No one shall know it was you."

Exhaustion suddenly swamped Lucian. A yawn rolled through him. He nodded to Zadon knowing that his life was safe in Zadon's hands. "Thanks brother."

He climbed into his bed as Zadon stood and wandered to the door. "I shall see you tomorrow, Lucian. It will be made clear in the morning."

As he dreamed, he was plagued by flashes of violence, the faces of the panther shifters haunting him. His body grew restless as he fought the recall of memories when a white light filled his mind. It shocked him. Never before had a dream been overtaken. Out of the blinding light came a gigantic wolf. It was black as the blackest night, swallowing the brilliance that heralded his arrival. Lucian's subconscious mind stared at the wolf. The wolf stared right back. It took a few moments before he spoke.

"Hello, my son."

Lucian swallowed his throat dry. "Hello."

"I wanted to personally welcome you to the role of Alpha. Each Alpha belonging to Baelia earns a direct connection to me. Do you know who I am?"

Lucian was floored. He was fairly certain who it was but was scared to voice the name. He stayed mute.

"I am Lord Culgan, God of the Wolves."

Lucian nodded numbly. "I am most blessed to be in your presence."

"I have more to tell you than just a welcome. We Gods have been stuck within the Void for a very long time. I fear we will never be able to leave. Yet, I am the only God that finds I still have some ability to affect the outcomes in Baelia. I must send you a warning meant for another in the hopes you can see it to the people most in need."

"What kind of help can I give?"

"You, my son, have all the power to help. There is a coup in the works, the target is the throne of Drakore. I need you to exercise your influence to save them." The wolf gave him a long look, his eyes sparkling like stars.

"You don't understand Lord Culgan, I don't have power. My own father doesn't even listen to me. How am I going to get another kingdom's royalty to listen?" He knew he should speak more carefully with a God however panic had his stomach clenching.

"Are you not betrothed to one of the daughters? Keep working with your father. You will see."

Lucian opened his mouth to retort but the God was gone.

Six

SUZU

PALION - BENE - YEAR 7557

Suzu gathered all the little bits of paper that cluttered her desk, organizing them into a somewhat more manageable pile. Harold was an annoying task master requiring reports every single day regardless of the actual goings on in the kingdom. Today however a change occurred. The ceremony of the Alpha had happened the night before and ended badly. At least for a few attendees.

The guards had found what could only be described as the remains of what was assumed to be three guests. Though it was nearly impossible to tell given what they found. Flesh scattered wide, a large pool of bodily fluid which unfortunately had been soaked into the ground, making it impossible to tell how much had been there originally. Bones were piled haphazardly around the hedges and by the Palace walls.

Suzu had been in disbelief when she heard the rumors from the palace guards, mainly from Ulfur her best friend, and in the early hours of the morning she had snuck out of her rooms to go look. The cleaners had been to the scene, the smell of scrubbing magic, overwhelming with lemon, thick in the air. Yet even though they had tried to right the terrible wrong, Suzu could still feel the disruption and violence that had happened. Her heart in her throat she did her duty, walking the entire scene, carefully noting all that seemed off. Her immediate feelings were jotted down in her notebook, all pointing toward the existence of a true evil within Palion that had yet to be discovered. She didn't relish the meeting that would have to happen now. Her steps were meandering and slow as she made her way down the hallway holding her note-book tight to her chest trying to stall the outrage.

Harold's study was right off the library, and Suzu always took care to linger amongst the books before slipping in the doors. Suzu had only been the spymaster for the last year. It had been decided that her position was to remain a secret from everyone in the court. Foregoing her place at the council meet-ings which was unusual from past spymasters, as far as anyone could guess Harold was running the kingdom without a one. She took the reins from her mentor Vig when he wanted to retire. Vig had found her love of puzzles and retention of facts essential to the job and had taken care in training her for the past few years. There had been a fight in front of them when it came to getting Harold to agree to her taking the position from Vig. He had fought hard, wanting Vig to train a man instead, believing wholeheartedly that women were too weak to do any job of importance. Suzu was fairly certain that if Vig had given in that man would have been allowed in council meetings. Suzu still wasn't sure what Vig did in the end to ensure she got the role, all she knew was an oath had been made. Vig still wore the mark on his neck as a stark reminder.

As she slipped through the doors Harold glanced up from his ornate desk and nodded once, immediately placing what-ever he was working on to the side. His office was luxury given physical form. The desk was large and intricately carved wood, the windows draped with heavy brocade curtains, often pulled closed. Candles littered every surface giving the needed light to continue with business as usual despite his insistence on blocking out the natural light. He made sure there was only one seat for visitors, and it was the most uncomfortable creation, so much so she was certain that was an intentional design. He crossed his hands in front of him and waited patiently for her to sit and divulge what she had learned over the past week.

Suzu bowed deeply before gingerly taking her seat across from him. She opened her notebook and flipped to the appropriate page. "This week the largest event that shook the kingdom was the passing over the Alphadom from the Elder to the Prince." Harold grunted acknowledgement but did not comment further. Suzu had hoped that he would use the blessing of the Alphadom as a way to get closer to his son and heir but if anything it had pushed them further apart. She sighed a bit before continuing her report.

"The ceremony went off without a hitch but there was one incident that was reported late last night. It appears that an attack occurred in the back rose gardens, three victims at best guess. It has been cleaned up for the most part, but it is unclear who holds the responsibility. I have begun seeking out sources and gone to investigate the site myself. It's a matter of time before we know the truth."

Harold straightened a bit. "What was the attack? Who was killed?"

"That is part of the mystery. We think there were at least two victims, but the guards argue over a possible third given the amount of bones left behind. The smell tells us they were panther shifters. No one has been reported missing so it's hard to tell. The remains were completely unrecognizable. The body or bodies of the victims were turned almost completely to liquid. We have found bits of bones piled around the hedges and against the wall but there was also a large remnant of a puddle. The bodily fluid has soaked into the ground so it's hard to see how much there was, to know how many victims."

Harold was nodding along tapping his chin. "How is this awareness going to help me? What should we do to better protect our people? Considering you have no actual clues or knowledge."

Suzu sighed, picking up the insult easily, "I would suggest you increase security on the grounds. We don't know if it was a wolf that did this. It is far from their usual style. If it was someone or something else, we need to be better prepared."

Harold inclined his head. "I shall use this as a teaching moment for Lucian. My oath requires me to raise him, so raise him I shall. It is time to see him demonstrate some of those leadership skills. Although I doubt he even has any."

Suzu held her tongue not wanting to further anger Harold, when it came to his own son, their relationship was already so tenuous.

SEVEN

HAROLD

PALION - BENE - YEAR 7557

Harold pulled out the letter he had kept in his top drawer for the last four months. Unwilling to acknowledge that things were changing and unsure how he wanted to move forward for the kingdom. Larial's words about loving her son rang in his head every time he read through the note. She wouldn't want him to hide this, she would want Lucian to have every opportunity to accept it on his own terms. Yet he knew Lucian. The conniving bastard that killed his own mother. He would find a way to ruin this, and they needed the Berrids to strengthen the powers against Dodsfell. Part of him wished he had never heard her thoughts of love, it would have made it much simpler to set the child aside, away from the looming power of the throne.

Good Evening, King Harold:
It is with a heavy heart I write to you needing

to change our previously agreed upon betrothal pact. Cerial is no longer available to fulfill her side of the obligation, however it is with the Gods blessing we offer to you, Aurelia. She is only two-years younger than her sister but just as beautiful. Her intelligence will go far in furthering your kingdom in the future. All we require is that she get a two-year extension to the marriage contract, to account for the age difference. I will send her to you after the two year extension with a full entourage, as was originally agreed upon for her sister. I shall take silence as your acceptance of this upgrade to the betrothal.

~Aydan, King of Drakore

Darkness swirled within the edges of his mind, always present and always being beaten back by the reality in which he lived. Suzu must have left as he read the letter, so he stood cracking the curtain, glancing down into the palace garden. If he squinted, he could almost see her walking through her precious flowers rubbing her belly. He sighed deeply, knowing he had to face his idiot son once again. The only thing that kept Lucian breathing was the blonde locks and green eyes so similar to his wife. He stuck his head out into the library and waved down a serving lad who was helping the librarian. "Go get my son. Bring him to me directly."

The serving lad stared at him, mouth agape. It took a sharp elbow from the elderly librarian to get the boy moving, but it seemed he moved with purpose.

Harold went back to his work debating the news he had received from Hesperdae and Aydan. Their desire to switch daughters on him was greatly disturbing. It just wasn't done. Once these arrangements were made and solidified by the Obas, they didn't just haphazardly change them. After all, it took time to get the children to agree in the first place. The term child was loosely made as both Cerial Berrid and his own son were past their eighteenth birthday. Yet as long as they listened to their parents', children they would be called.

He was shocked at the prompt timing, as a knock sounded on the door right before it cracked open. Lucian peered inside a look of insolence apparent on his face.

"You summoned me."

"I did. I wanted you to hear the latest news. I also have a gift for you to celebrate your new station." He set his quill aside and looked expectantly at Lucian gesturing him to take a seat.

Lucian stepped further into the room. Harold suppressed the urge to roll his eyes as he noticed the tenuous quality to his steps. As if afraid of walking all the way into the chamber. *Why didn't this child have a backbone?* Once Lucian was seated in the chair Suzu had so recently vacated, Harold took a deep breath.

"As Alpha you will receive many honors, I am sure. I wanted to be sure I was the one to bestow upon you the first." He waved away the importance as if it was a normal occurrence, not wanting to bring any sort of notice to his kindness.

"You didn't have to." Harold was pleased to see the discomfort evident upon Lucian's face.

"No I didn't. But I did it nonetheless." He held up a finger stemming off the flow of words from Lucian. "Best let me tell you what the honor is before you go sending me all the praise." He paused making sure Lucian complied, "I am placing you and your wolves, I'll even let you decide which wolf, in charge of security. I have had a report of an attack on the palace grounds that occurred last night during your ceremony. Doubtless you were too distracted to notice. However, we cannot let violence continue inside the premises."

He watched Lucian taking note of the emotions that flipped across his face. One aspect of his lovely wife that Lucian had inherited was her inability to hide emotions. Lucian was quite obviously very confused and upset by the news. He made a vain attempt to counsel his face to neutrality, but Harold decided now was better than ever to let the final hammer drop. "The last thing I need you to know is that your betrothal to Cerial Berrid has been canceled."

Lucian met his gaze, a fleeting look of hope sparked within his eyes.

Harold could feel the smile he meant to convey come off more as a sneer. "Don't get too excited lad. You are now betrothed to Aurelia Berrid. The younger of the Berrid girls."

Lucian swallowed back a retort. Instead he managed to shock Harold. "I have been informed that there is a coup brewing in Drakore. Perhaps we should lend them our aid. Help solidify the betrothal and the future wellbeing of my bride-to-be."

Harold blinked. "A coup is brewing in Drakore boy?"

"Yes, Sir. I was warned that we need to help them if we are able to."

Harold began to laugh. "And where in the world are you getting your sources?"

Lucian swallowed hard. "I was told by the Gods."

Harold began to laugh in earnest, his breath coming in wheezes. He began to cough as he straightened up. "The Gods chose you? The weakest Prince in the history of our pitiful kingdom. We have nothing to snag the Gods attention nor does Drakore so why, why would they deign to talk to either of our kingdoms?"

Lucian stood abruptly, bowing sharply. "My duty has been administered. I shall see to the safety of the palace grounds. The plan will be delivered to you by the end of the week."

Harold was still chuckling as Lucian walked out of the room, his back iron rod straight. Harold pulled out a fresh piece of paper and began to scribble down a note for Suzu written in a code taught to him by Vig.

Look into the stability of the crown in Drakore. The tide may be turning.

He stuck his head out and got another serving lad to deliver the note to Suzu.

eight

LUCIAN

PALION - BENE - YEAR 7557

> Demons have a vast array of power potential. An individual demon is limited however, to what the God Tixdarr gives them. Most commonly demons get a smattering of small powers such as, invisibility and basic levitation. As a demon ages and goes through the hierarchy they are able to petition for greater more complex magics such as mind reading and conjuring. It is rare but not unheard of, that a demon can tap into the power of the elements. Any demon worth its mettle keeps a lid on the full extent of his power lest someone smarter use them against him.
>
> ~Tixdarr Temple Archives

Lucian stomped down the marble hallway from the library as frustration filled his every footfall. He headed down to the eastern tower which held a smaller conference room alongside a bunch of rooms capable of being used as studies. Zadon stepped from a shadowy doorway joining him in silence as they made their way toward Lucian's chosen sanctum.

"Send out a notice to Ulfur. From all the talking happening in my head and from what the Elder told me he is the best warrior among the wolves."

Lucian caught the quizzical look Zadon sent him and ignored it shoving his way through the oak door. He threw himself into a chair looking absently out the window. *His father would never understand him. He would never truly love him. Why had it taken him eighteen years for that to sink in?* This gift could barely be seen as a gift, it was more like an added responsibility coupled with a test he was sure to fail.

Lucian scrubbed at his face. His mind racing at the injustices. He should get more responsibility in the kingdom, but it should have been accompanied with training. He had no other options available to him but to listen to his instincts, no matter how broken they might be, the wolves had to be where the answers lay.

A knock sounded from the doorway distracting Lucian from his thoughts, pulling his attention back to the room. "Come in."

A man tall enough that he filled the entryway to such an extent he shadowed the room, stood there waiting patiently. Lucian knew he was a wolf, his own, scenting their pack bond. The man who had to be Ulfur, administered a deep bow before approaching the desk settling into a chair opposite Lucian.

Lucian's eyes darted between Zadon and Ulfur, unsure what to do next. He had never had the opportunity to lead anyone except Zadon, and that was more of a friendship. Zadon, frustratingly unhelpful, took up a guard stance against the wall near the door, a smirk on his face. *Right now is the time to show great leadership skills.*

He cleared his throat and gave Ulfur what he hoped was a warm smile. "Do you all know each other?"

The men glanced at one another awkwardly before the wolf shrugged, "I've heard the rumors." He glanced at Zadon and back to Lucian.

Lucian flushed a bit, "I am not sure what the rumors are." He gestured at Zadon. "Regardless this is Zadon, one of my closest friends and advisors." He looked at the wolf standing in front of his desk. "This is Ulfur." They both grunted merely nodding in each other's direction.

He shifted uncomfortably in his chair before once more clearing his throat. "I have a need to increase my court. I have been charged with the protection of the palace and those inside it." Ulfur crossed his arms, a look of intrigue flashing on his face. "A situation occurred last night that has put security in question. I would need you to take over ensuring that there were warriors doing patrols, along with coming up with plans for if someone were to invade."

Ulfur nodded a bit, "Will I be able to hire on who I need to help me? Or are you interested in approving any appointments?"

Zadon's voice cracked out harsh and unforgiving, "Who do you need? If you're as great a warrior as they claim, you should be able to handle it yourself."

Ulfur's jaw clenched, and Lucian inwardly groaned. "As amazing as I am, it's important to have two shifts of guards, morning and night. Perhaps you can survive without sleep, but I am man enough to admit that it isn't the case for me."

Lucian stood, breaking the tension. "Ulfur you may hire whoever you want, however I ask you to give Zadon the name so he can check into them. That way you both are happy."

Ulfur nodded. "Alright, that works for me. I would love to serve the Alpha in this manner."

Lucian smiled widely, confidence filling him in his role as Alpha. "Excellent. Due to your new status you qualify for quarters in the palace. Just let the housekeeper know and he will assign them to you."

"I grew up around the palace. My father is a member of your father's guard. Once I was grown, I had to move to the bunk house so it will be nice to work with Rusk to establish my own residence here."

Lucian flushed a bit, put off that he hadn't known that Ulfur lived his entire life on the grounds. *How had that happened? How did he not know?* Visions of his childhood flashed through his mind. Locked doors. Silent rooms. Flying belts. Angry screams. He had not been allowed to wander through the palace even though he would one day inherit it.

Lucian held his hand out, relief flooding through him when Ulfur grasped it firmly. Ulfur bowed once again before heading out undoubtedly to start his new role. A deep sigh escaped Lucian as he slumped back into his chair, wiping his sweaty palms on his thighs. He groaned a bit at the smirk on Zadon's face. "What did I do wrong?"

"Well sire, that was a bit, awkward." He walked around the desk opening the bottom drawer and pulling out the dark amber liquor that Lucian kept there. Zadon poured a hefty helping proffering it to Lucian. "You need to learn how to address those that are lesser than you. After all you are a Prince of the blood of Palion. That deserves respect, you will only get respect if you treat those around you according to their stations in life. You were far too friendly."

Lucian rolled his eyes in exasperation at the expectation that existed around him. "That means I don't get to have friends. You do realize that right?"

"An unfortunate reality of your Princely status." Zadon shrugged indifferently "You'll always have me."

Lucian rubbed at his temples and shook his head. "I need to be able to be myself here. That doesn't mean I don't appreciate you, but I have to find a way to navigate this my way."

Zadon inclined his head with a smile. "Of course, sire. Whatever you think is appropriate."

nine

SUZU

PALION - XITA - YEAR 7557

Suzu looked down at the note from her top informant. *This can't be correct.* She had seen top units of the Drakore military conducting maneuvers in the neutral land between the two kingdoms. She clucked her tongue against the roof of her mouth. The ruling family seemed to be large and in charge, yet why was the military conducting maneuvers in the neutral lands? That was a red flag that needed further attention, she carefully drew a star denoting the importance.

She had done as Harold had demanded and sent operatives out to take account of the state of Drakore. As far as most of them could tell everything was normal. The youngest girl, Lucian's new betrothed bride had been sent to the Crowlands for Queen training. It raised Suzu's eyebrows because why wouldn't they train a queen in the palace, however it wasn't egregious enough to flag for Harold's perusal. Merely a puzzle piece to set aside for now.

Familiar with Harold's need for extreme detail Suzu had

gone above and beyond, preemptively sending an operative into the jungle of the mountains to lay eyes upon Aurelia. She hadn't expected that operative to fail so miserably, they had somehow gotten so turned around that they were scared to push onward, instead opting to return to Palion.

The process of establishing the strength of their neighbors had taken a few weeks of time and the stress was starting to show. She had been struggling lately in keeping her cover intact. The gossips and rumor mongers were out for her blood because, they existed in a twisted world where she had to fit the life *they* envisioned appropriate for one in the court.

She had grown up in the Palion palace, her father a high-ranking courtier. Yet, as she aged it was expected that she would marry and produce heirs for her husband. Much of the court assumed her father was merely allowing her a few years of freedom before forcing her into an advantageous match. What they didn't realize is she called the shots. Her people, panther shifters, were a matriarchal bunch and when her mother passed into the Void it fell on her to create plans for the family. For now she merely allowed the court to believe what they wanted as she spent her days indulging in charities which happened to be overseen directly by the King.

What no one but the King understood was that Palion benefited by her not marrying. All of her energy centered so heavily on progressing the kingdom that she had no time for a partner, which also meant that she never encountered the right set of circumstances to find her soulbond. At one point she had thought it would be Ulfur, so much so she had started cultivating a mental cache for all the secrets she dealt with. Yet, when she turned eighteen and sought him out, the pull she'd always felt remained the same, no different than before. It was clear that they both were disappointed by the lack of a bond, but they never pushed to find out why. If the stories were true, Soulbonds would feel a click when the right one came along, disappointedly the mental click hadn't happened after their birthdays.

She sighed, a glance outside told her she would be lucky to get to her meeting on time. She stood and made her way to the library pulling out a book at random about the psychology of shifters and their various shapes. It would be a reasonable distraction should someone question her, her little mice had told her that Zadon liked to ask questions about her after he caught her coming from meetings with the King. The more interest he directed at her, the more she turned back onto him, eager, for more dirt to use against the slimy demon.

She knocked on the King's study and slipped inside after hearing the gruff, "Enter."

She curtsied low before taking her seat, arranging her note-book. "The Berrids appear strong and all powerful. There is but one small deviation, it appears that Rayner Svenston, the Military General of Drakore, has broken from Aydan's over-sight. He is exercising the military in the neutral lands far from any supervision."

"Hmm." Harold tapped the desk staring off into the distance. "I see. I suppose we could warn them. It would be the neighborly thing to do. Although it would also be inter-esting to see the Berrids scramble for once. I would pay a pretty silver to see Hesper's face at the news, that's for sure, the bitch doesn't know her place. What of this new daughter?"

"She's two years younger than Lucian and Cerial. Seem-ingly she's the hot head of the family but we were unable to actually appraise her looks, though it is rumored she takes after Aydan's coloring with raven hair and the sky-blue eyes." She shrugged a bit.

"Why were you unable to have someone lay their eyes on her? Where is she exactly?" She watched as Harold leaned closer intent on her answer.

"She has been sent to the Crowlands, for training in preparation for her new position. It is said that Cerial went to the Crowlands around the time her betrothal was originally announced. Perhaps there's a ceremony that happens there. My operative attempted to locate these lands but got lost in the jungles of the mountains."

"Interesting. So they sent her to the famed Crowlands. The home of Hesper, a place acclaimed to be highly beautiful and treacherous for the non-flyer."

"Overall though your tip on them being in danger seems to be unfounded. They merely need to lock up that wayward General of theirs and any uprising should be cut off at the knees."

Harold nodded. "I shall take this under advisement. Once again you exceed my expectations of what you can do. I have given my son a job within the palace, and he has chosen to elevate that friend of yours. The big one."

Suzu straightened a bit. A small frown on her face. "Ulfur?"

"Yes, that's the one. Yes, you both were rambunctious growing up, making it clear how strict I needed to be with Lucian to keep him from acting like that. Anyway you need to use your relationship with that large wolf boy, get closer to Lucian and drive him away from the demon. That slimy demon is the one mistake I have made in all these years since Larial died. Lucian is too weak to withstand the demon's manipulative ways, with that monster by his side he will never be ready. I don't currently have another option other than Lucian, so you need to fix the situation."

"I don't." Suzu began her objections, but the King held up his hand.

"Ah, ah, ah, we don't need to hear any womanly objections now. You signed up to be my spymaster's apprentice willingly enough, nor did you object when he handed over the job to you. Now you will do the next logical step and actually spy yourself, telling me exactly what my son is up to in his little pretend court."

Suzu flushed, anger and indignation heating her skin. "I see. The problem is that *if* they are up to something you want ceased it will become abundantly obvious that I am the mole, or that Ulfur is. Which puts us both in harm's way. I refuse to place him in danger, let alone myself."

She stood her limbs shaking as anger overtook fear. The King chuckled. "I suppose if that were to happen you failed at your training. We shall see which is true, either you were made to do this job or you're just a woman pretending to be useful."

Not waiting for her formal dismissal she stomped out of the room.

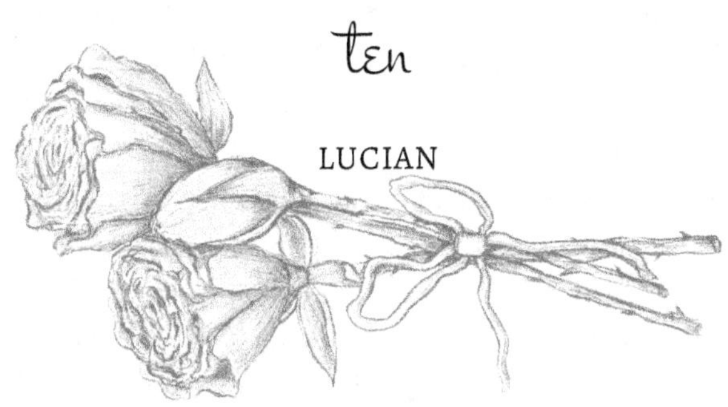

ten

LUCIAN

PALION - XITA - YEAR 7557

The sun setting sent bright colors throughout his living area which helped distract from the obvious

"Sire, I think you need to look into a different wolf. Ulfur isn't up to the task as head of the Palace Guard."

Lucian gripped hard to his patience, rubbing his temple. Zadon hadn't even given Ulfur a full month to settle into the job before demanding a change. "Why Zadon?"

"He is proving his ineptitude daily! Have you seen the latest?"

"I see a man working hard to organize a group of volunteers. He has managed to get them into shifts and training to be better. He also has done it in such a small amount of time." Part of him cursed his father, gathering palace guards and training them should have been undertaken years ago. Yet, Harold had rested on the idea that the Great Power would protect them. Drakore and the impending coup was proof enough that the Great Powers weren't infallible.

"He had to hire a second. He couldn't figure out how to

do it on his own. He should give up the position to a man better capable." Lucian noted the stubborn set of Zadon's jaw and realized what was happening.

"Zadon you're not less important to me just because you aren't the head of my guard. I will find you a better fit within the court. It just hasn't appeared yet. Leave Ulfur to his position." Zadon met his gaze, and Lucian could see him wrestling with acceptance.

"Fine." Zadon stomped past Lucian, heading for the drink cupboard. "Let's drink to my future post then."

Lucian heard the clinking of glass against glass and accepted the brown liquor readily enough. He looked at it and his mind reeled back, something inside begging him to not drink. On top of the brown liquid swirled a multicolored sheen. "Uhh, Zadon what is in this?"

"It's just liquor. Look, we can switch glasses." Lucian did but was disturbed to see the sheen was still in Zadon's glass.

Lucian picked up the glass looking at the liquid from all angles, even bringing it up high in front of the window to see if the sun illuminated the cause of the sheen. Skepticism coated his tongue, "Perhaps it's just the washing of the glasses. I'll have to talk to Rusk about it, he will make sure the maids rinse the glasses more thoroughly." He took a swig. The flavor the same as every other time they had partook. Tension built in his shoulders, his body preparing for a fight with an unknown opponent. Oil began to ooze around his soul, reminding him of the Alpha ceremony. Fear gripped his mind.

Since that horrible night his mind had created a shield over the essential parts of himself that made him Lucian, with his wolf standing guard ready to fight the oily evil slinking through his veins. Yet as the days passed, turning into weeks the inner protection weakened, cracks easily seen. Tendrils of inky blackness shot out aiming for those weak spots, his wolf biting and snarling at them until they disappeared.

"You have to fight it Lucian, fight with me"

The order came out as a demand, causing pain to sear across his temple. Lucian rubbed at it doing his best to shore up his mental defenses. Zadon stepped closer to the desk undoubtedly noting the change in demeanor. "Zadon something's wrong. Pain. So much pain."

Lucian pulled both his hands up, but the movement became more difficult, his arms not listening to him. He opened his mouth to exclaim, to explain the difficulties to Zadon but he found his tongue not working properly. It felt thick and dry, unable to move, to form the much-needed words to portray what he required.

Lucian was trapped within his mind as he listened to a deeper darker voice emerge from his own mouth. "Administer pain."

Lucian registered the confusion and delight that crossed Zadon's face as he rushed to Lucian's side. The world became blurry, and dark as his body followed Zadon's. It took a few minutes before Lucian gained a semblance of control over his own eyes, able to see the darkened cobblestones dripping with water, algae green and slimy growing along the edges.

What are we doing in the dungeons?

It became obvious almost as soon as the thought left his mind what they were doing. A bound and gagged individual seemed to be tied to the wall. Lucian's internal self-reeled at the prospect of what was going to happen. That momentary flinch was all that was needed for the black to take full control locking Lucian out of every sense he once knew.

eleven

ZADON

PALION - XITA - YEAR 7557

The cobbled stone room covered in dank algae, smelled strongly of dirt and mold as they entered. The smell of piss and blood lingered in the corners and became more clear the farther into the room they went. Zadon had prepared this specific room for the next step in the experiment and eagerness that his plan was coming to fruition bubbled within. Zadon watched Lucian carefully as he took in the sight of the dangling man, the final light of softness extinguished from behind his eyes. Instead all that dwelled in the depths of Lucian's emerald eyes was darkness, devoid of all emotions.

Zadon pulled the cover off a rack of weaponry. He watched as Lucian's attention caught and held onto the shiny weapons. Lucian lumbered, his steps staggered and awkward as he picked up one particular whip which had a thrill shooting through Zadon. The star pointed whip was designed for nothing more than the administering of pain. A slow death where the flesh would leisurely ripped away. Zadon had seen it used extensively in Dodsfell and most of the time, when artfully wielded the recipient of the lash would end up with his bones exposed before death finally graced him.

Lucian's body cracked the whip a few times as if getting a feel for the weight and heft. Zadon couldn't tear his eyes away as the new and improved Lucian looked at the prisoner. "Go forth and administer his punishment sire."

He had opted to leave the prisoner gagged, unsure if the sounds of screaming would jar Lucian back into control. It would take experimentation to see how much control the darkness truly had on Lucian's mind. It was a delicate balance, wanting to push the violence while remaining close to the weakling prince in order to stay safe within Palion and Baelia at large.

The lash flew hitting the man being held up by just his wrists. The impact causing the prisoner's body to swing violently from left to right. Lucian waited the few minutes it took for the body to quit swaying before unleashing another swing. Zadon stood amazed that it only took two swings for flesh to start stripping away. The body again swung for a few minutes.

Zadon tapped Lucian's shoulder, "A minute sire. I shall affix him so he no longer swings."

"Where are the screams?"

Zadon looked to the floor hiding the glee that swarmed within at the prospect that next time there would be more violence. He bowed submissively toward Lucian. "Sire I was caught off guard and this man is under a sleeping draft. However, next time I will ensure they are awake and twitching."

He scurried closer to the prisoner using the manacle that encompassed the prisoner's ankles to secure him to the ground. Once that was done, he stepped back taking in the blood pooling on the ground from the cuts in the prisoners back. Zadon watched Lucian carefully noticing that the dark dead void was still in place within his eyes as he let loose once more.

The lashings kept coming without breaks. Zadon kept count as the tenth lash flew and the last vestiges of flesh fell from the prisoners back. It seemed to Zadon that Lucian's arm was moving slower, more staggered.

He took it as his sign that the internal battle was raging once more. Zadon touched Lucian's shoulder moving slowly to take the whip from Lucian's hand. He removed the whip and forced Lucian's body around. Dropping the whip he gently urged Lucian out of the dungeon room. Before leading Lucian back up towards his bedchamber Zadon took care to lock the room behind them.

He would have to get rid of the body at some point and couldn't risk someone walking in on the mess. He moved toward Lucian's body, seemingly frozen, going to the trouble to propel him forward towards his room away from possible prying eyes.

twelve

SUZU

PALION - XITA - YEAR 7557

> Shifters of the land exist within most animal species. For example not all tigers are shifters but those that are tend to emulate the characteristics common with the tiger they can become. In the Kingdom of Palion these creatures tend to work well together. The headstrong creatures tend to rule more often than not. The food chain exists even for shifters, a mouse will never be able to rule the kingdom.
>
> ~Palion Archives

An exasperated sigh left her as she spread out the various notes across the top of her desk. She strummed her fingers against the wood, thinking hard. *How did this happen again?* The king had mandated Lucian create a security team to make the Palace and palace grounds secure. Which he had done. She knew that for a fact because Ulfur had become the leader of said group. He loved to expound on the various activities he had set for his underlings even going as far as hiring on a panther shifter as his second to prove he cared for more than just the wolves. Her face warmed a bit at the possibility he had done that for her. Honoring that she wasn't a wolf like so many of their friends.

Yet again a month or so after the first instance another body had been found. It wasn't the exact same, so it would be hard to say if the killer had indeed been the same person. The victim had died a violent death but at least they could tell that they had been a shifter instead of a pile of mush and bits. He had been whipped, his skeleton exposed, obviously having experienced great pain before Tixdarr took his soul. *How was it missed? How did the patrols not hear it?*

A hum left her throat as she debated all the possibilities. Someone close to the security team, in the guard or in the court must be involved with the violence. *Yet who?*

She glanced out the window and took note that it was about time she made her way to her meeting with the King. The meetings had become more stilted and uncomfortable, yet she rolled her shoulders ready to face the music.

As she left her rooms she made full body contact with a soft wall. She stuttered back barely catching herself before falling backwards, glancing up she saw it was Ulfur. Ire sparked that he was in her way adding to the anxiety that she was late. "Watch where you're going!"

Ulfur reached out, though he was too far to effectively aid in catching her had she actually fallen. "Sorry Kitten. I was just looking for you. I know you've been scared about the attacks."

She swallowed her retort wanting to defend herself. She wasn't truly scared. Times like this her job of being a spymaster wore on her spirit, she didn't want to seem inept or scared when she rarely was. She just needed to know what was happening for her job. Let whoever was responsible meet her in a dark alley they would be surprised at their reception.

She blinked, pulling forth fake fear from her mind's well-spring of emotions, lowering her eyes and letting her lip tremble, a common trick for spies in the field. "Yes, it is rather frightening to hear about the atrocities that have happened so close to our home. Is the palace even safe?!"

Ulfur's chest puffed up as he stepped closer grabbing at her free hand. "Absolutely you are safe. Remember I am in charge of the warriors. The bastard only got one this time and there won't be a next time. I promise that." Suzu heavily resisted the eye roll that wanted to slip forward.

It was clear she had run into Ulfur because he was seeking her out for some reason. "What did you want to tell me so swiftly, Ulfur? I am rather late for a charity meeting."

"Oh yes! I needed to warn you because I knew you were rather scared about this whole ordeal. We have found out why no one heard the victim shouting. The victim was more than likely drugged. The medical team thinks it was a sleeping draft. So be wary of drinking things that you don't prepare yourself for the time being."

Her interest peaked. This was actually helpful news that would go a bit farther to keeping the King off his lectures on her ineptitude at least for a little bit. "Wow! You may be good at your job after all you, big lug."

"Hey! I thought you gave up that nickname when we were kids." Ulfur scowled a bit causing Suzu to lose grip on her forced fear.

"Ahh well nicknames never truly die do they?" She grinned at him as she stepped around him waving back cheekily.

thirteen

HAROLD

PALION - XITA - YEAR 7557

He slammed his fist down on his desk, causing it to vibrate in protest, anger radiating through him. "WHY are there bodies being found on the palace grounds?"

Harold watched his son twitch at the impact, "I have yet to see the report father. You called me in before I had a chance to meet with my Generals."

"If you are going to run this kingdom, in any capacity, at any point in the future, you should have already known about the body! How can I train you to take power? Why should I trust you? I should find a fosterling and train him over you. You have been lucky so far Lucian. I was going to do this years ago but got distracted."

Lucian's jaw tightened and Harold held his breath hoping that his son would break control just once and try something. Attempt to push back. Prove his worth. Yet it seemed like Lucian's weak side was still in control.

"I shall meet with my Generals and make sure we double the patrols. I appreciate you letting me know the problem and I will now address it. Keep in mind if you do replace me you will have a hard time controlling the wolves, as will your heir." Lucian stood and walked toward the door.

Harold began to laugh. "I see. I will let you know when I have your brother picked out. I'm sure I can find a fosterling in need with more suitable morals to run a kingdom. If you can't understand how to keep the palace safe, I'll just replace you. Regardless of what the wolves want, they are after all merely one species within this kingdom." He watched Lucian roll his shoulders walking out of the study.

fourteen

LUCIAN

PALION - XITA - YEAR 7557

He slammed the door of his office the figures on his bookshelf, undoubtedly picked out by Rusk ages ago, shook dangerously in response. Lucian opened his mouth, screaming out his frustration. Unsure what to do with his pent-up anger towards his father. He heard but did not acknowledge Zadon's entrance. He doubled over his blood roaring in his ears, his breathing shallow.

Zadon approached and sat down. "What did your father say?"

"He thinks he can replace me. He thinks he can go get a new son and train him to be the heir. I cannot get a handle on the security, so I am failing. If I fail I lose. If I continue to lose I will be gone." His teeth ground together causing an ache to form behind his jaw.

"How exactly is he proposing to replace you?" Zadon tapped his fingers together waiting.

Lucian stood straighter and paced toward the window.

"He will find a fosterling and train them to be me. To take the responsibility of prince and heir. I will disappear." He ran his hands through his hair trying to figure out what to do. "Where are Ulfur and Juro?"

Zadon sat up straighter, "I believe they are at the guard house. They were both on shift last night."

"They were on shift?! Why didn't they tell us about the body?" He pulled his hair, anger settling deeper into his bones.

Zadon shrugged. "Perhaps they don't trust you enough to tell you the truth. It's hard for some men to open up to authority figures when all they have is bad news to circulate."

Incredulity spread through Lucian as he turned back to Zadon raising an eyebrow in question. "Weren't you the one who told me to be more a Prince, less of a friend? Now you think I need to be closer to them. Do you even know what you're talking about?"

He watched Zadon nod wincing a bit at his point. "I shall go and get them, perhaps they can explain themselves adequately."

The sound of the door opening allowing his friend to leave on his errand barely registered in his ears. His mind spiraling as the clock ticked down. It felt like hours of pacing, his feet wearing the floor out before the window as he flipped through all the possible ways the killer could have succeeded. The fact that whomever killed the man did so by gaining access to the grounds without a singular guard noticing anything suspicious had his mind twisting into knots.

Ulfur entered first followed closely by Juro, Lucian didn't cease his movements until Zadon dramatically slammed the door closed behind all of them. The room fell silent, the only true sound was the scrap of his boots against the tiled floor, everyone's body seemed to radiate tension and anger. Lucian couldn't cap the words any longer, "Why is it I was notified by the King that there was a body found last night? Why didn't you report to me? You are my court! Beholden to *me*, not him! I should have been the first to know." He slammed his fist on the desk and then quickly turned punching the window furious that he had mimicked his horrific father. Glass shattered and tinkled as it fell to the ground. His fist stinging with the tiny cuts.

Juro cleared his throat sitting straighter. "The body wasn't present when we turned over the guard duty patrol near dawn. The best I can come up with is that someone knows our routines and snuck the body out during the change."

Ulfur stared daggers at Lucian before adding, "Perhaps it means that the damage was done elsewhere. The area he was found in was remarkably clean. No gore or blood stain to be found. Highly unusual for how he died."

"How did he die?"

"The King didn't say?" Ulfur toed the line of challenge and Lucian could feel it. Yet he couldn't call him out on it directly, not until he was assured it would not lead to more trouble.

Lucian's lip peeled upward as he snarled. "No he didn't." He could feel his wolf close to the surface for the first time since the Alpha ceremony. It reminded him that his wolfs presence felt truly magical and it prompted an internal question on where his wolf had been.

Ulfur had the good graces to look down, shame emanating from him. A small whine emerging as his wolf recognized the Alpha in Lucian.

Juro broke the tension. "He was lashed to death, Your Highness."

Lucian felt the blood flood out of his face. There was a flash of a darkened room, a star pointed whip, before his memory went dark once more, nothing else came but horror settled into his soul. He darted a glance up at Zadon. A coldness settling into his chest, "Lashed? To what extent?"

Ulfur cleared his throat. "I can show you sire. Our wolves can connect, and you can see my memory of us reviewing the body."

Lucian nodded numbly. "Do it."

Lucian closed his eyes, reaching with a bit more ease than previously, for his wolf, and through that he could see a distorted image of a body. It had been lashed to the bone on the back, obviously drained of blood during the attack. Yet, no blood was presented on the ground where the body laid.

Lucian opened his eyes, taking a deep breath his nerves shot. A part of him recognized the man. It was the same one he had seen in his nightmare from last night. He met Zadon's eyes doing his best to control the terror that filled him, locking it within. Lucian turned back to Ulfur, "Thank you Ulfur, this is what we do next. We arrange it so that there is no time that someone can sneak into the grounds. Stagger the guard schedules so someone is always on duty. Recruit where we need from the city or the pack. The more wolves and panthers we have the more powerful we look." Both men nodded.

"Lastly, I want us to go out. The four of us specifically. There should be a bond between us where you feel comfortable coming to me with whatever you have, good or bad. Let's begin building that."

Ulfur and Juro exchanged looks and hesitatingly nodded agreement.

Lucian plowed past the hesitation. "Alright we will meet in the lobby tonight at sundown to go burn off some steam. Off you go to solidify those guard schedules."

As soon as they left the room Lucian turned to Zadon. "What is happening with me?"

"What do you mean sire?"

"I recognized that man. I saw him in my nightmares last night."

"You did? How surprising. What was the nightmare?"

Zadon inclined his head, if anyone else had looked at him in the same manner Lucian would say it was almost predatorily, but it was Zadon his friend and companion.

"I was feeling odd, and then I was in the dungeons, and then I saw that man, but I blacked out before I could see much more."

Zadon nodded understandingly. "Perhaps you only think you saw his face, because of his horrific circumstance so close to your nightmare. You know I have heard of a power that can project you into another's mind. Perhaps you found yourself doing that with the killer?"

Lucian screwed up his face considering. "Perhaps."

fifteen

LUCIAN

PALION - XITA - YEAR 7557

Lucian looked at the brick road in front of the palace, doing his best to not dwell over stress that came with making new friends. The only person he could reasonably call a friend was Zadon and he hadn't had to do anything to create the friendship. Zadon had showed up one day with his father and had attached himself to Lucian without any question. *What if they didn't come?* Making friends was hard for everyone, making friends with a grand title and the annoyance of being the supervisor made the task nearly impossible. The boots of the men sounded in the doorway as everyone gathered behind him. He took a deep breath and looking back at them with an affixed fake bravado, "I'm thinking Lykos would be a great place to drink our cares away." The men all whooped in excitement.

Lykos Pub was situated right at the base of Palace hill, making it the easiest pub for Lucian to escape to. The ride echoed with silence, all that could be heard was the heavy breathing and shifting within the seat. Lucian kept his smile fixed on his face nodding to anyone who met his gaze but unsure what to say to fill the empty air. The ride was short and bumpy but once the carriage came to a full stop, they all pushed out, eager to escape the suffocating silence for the loud music of a pub. He had visited Lykos a few times, due to its loud and crowded nature it was rare anyone noticed him as the heir apparent. He was instead allowed to just be Lucian. The feeling of being accepted filled him with a gratitude he couldn't put into words.

The main room was dark and dingy, the sticky floor leaving doubts on the cleanliness, nonetheless it felt warm and welcoming much like he thought a home should. All of a sudden, his wolf sat up inside alert and eager, fully commanding his attention. He felt his shoulders go stiff and his feet seemed glued to the residue slicked floor while his brain tried to process what had just happened. Ulfur, having caught on to the tension that filled Lucian's body threw an arm around his shoulder, "Where is she, my lord?"

Confusion fogged his mind. "Who? What's happening?"

Ulfur beamed at him, "Your wolf is alert right now, right? He's sensing a female. A good female, perhaps even *the female*. Now to figure out which one caught his attention." As Ulfur turned his attention to the crowded room Lucian pondered his words. *A female. His soulbond? Or just any female?*

He turned his head back to Ulfur, "Wait what," The words died on his lips as his eyes connected with hers.

She was a curvy brunette, curls of hair cascading all the way down her back in waves he wanted to run his hands through. Her caramel skin was flawless, a glow making her stand out from the crowded room. Everything radiated perfection. His feelings were solidified when she turned and he caught sight of her face, the deep green eyes, her mouth forming the perfect smile.

They locked eyes and his wolf howled. *Mate!* The word echoing through his mind.

His mouth fell open, the idea of finding a soulbond had never occurred to him. Ulfur let out a howl of joy, his wolf picking up what was happening between Lucian and the female across the room. Juro and Zadon came around questioning looks on their faces. Lucian however didn't tear his eyes from the girl. She met his gaze blushing as she took in the display near the door. He elbowed Ulfur in the ribs hoping to encourage him to shut up.

"Let's get a table." Zadon took control of the situation by corralling Ulfur and Juro toward the back bar. Lucian could feel his scrutiny but didn't look at him. Instead he took a deep breath opting to seek out the company of the mystery woman across the room, the desire to know her strong.

He forced his steps to be unhurried as he dodged bodies and came face to face with the gorgeous woman who he had somehow known about just by merely stepping into the same space as her. She was busily talking to a friend, a blonde who was cute but did not hold a candle to her.

"Hi."

She giggled. "Hello."

He bowed to her, the courtly manners that had been drilled into him his entire life taking hold, as he held out his hand for her to take.

"What?" She looked confused and her friend leaned in whispering in her ear causing the girl to blush and giggle. "Oh."

She took his hand and he could have sworn electricity shot through her fingertips into his own. It ricocheted around him and his wolf grew ever stronger the longer he held onto her.

He felt a tapping on his mind, and felt Ulfur's overbearing personality whisper through, *Invite her friend to the table please.*

Lucian couldn't help the chuckle that emerged as he turned toward the blonde. "Would you be interested in accompanying us? My friend would love to meet you." He pointed toward the table and the overeager Ulfur who was eyeing them intently.

The blonde laughed out loud at the look of pleading on Ulfur's face nodding her assent.

"Come let's introduce you to the group." He led both ladies across the room to the table where his Generals had settled. Lucian leaned over and whispered in her ear. "Do you want the chair?"

She pulled back enough to grin at him. "You look like you could be a chair in the right situation," She pushed him lightly causing him to sit in the only open chair. "There now you are ready for me." She sat down on his lap gently, he could tell she was pulling her weight as if concerned she was too heavy. He chuckled deeply pulling her into his chest. Something similar was happening with the blonde and Ulfur who was wrapping his arms around her lap, there was a random woman on Juro's lap but Zadon stood against the wall looking rather bored by all the displays of affection.

"Looks like we need to find you a woman Z!" He had to shout to be heard over the music.

Zadon sneered at the group. "No, no, my lord I wouldn't want one of those long term. Perhaps for an evening or two but nothing more than that."

Lucian laughed a bit before turning his attention to the lady who was nestled in his arms laughing at her friend. "So the man currently admiring your friend is Ulfur. Juro has a lady on his lap though I don't know her name. The sullen man holding up the wall is Zadon." *Best to not mention titles not yet.* He nuzzled into her neck, shocked that it felt so natural. He whispered into her ear. "What is your name?"

She turned in his lap and nuzzled into his own neck before

sitting up a bit looking at him. "My name is Kasria Lykos. Shouldn't you have asked that before walking me over to your friends?"

He grinned. "Perhaps. Yet this was more entertaining, right?"

She returned his grin with one of her own, "Yes, I suppose. Plus Belvina is surely having a great time with your friend."

Lucian dared a glance at Ulfur and the blonde laughing at the sight of the burly warrior practically hanging off of the petite blonde's words. "Do you want a drink or perhaps you want to dance with me." He whispered the question in her ear taking liberties even he was shocked by, being led by his wolf's demand. He nipped at her ear lobe.

She let out a breathy gasp, "A dance sounds good." She looked at him with half lidded eyes. As he pulled her onto the dance floor his mind started to kick on. *Should he trust her? Should he tell her the truth?* She looped her arms around his neck, her body swaying to the beat. He hadn't ever been very great at dancing, but he let the music take control of his body.

Kasria was talented, her luscious body draping easily over his, following his lead. It was thrilling that she seemed to be fully focused on him, not on his title, not on what she may get from him. Just him. For him. Too quickly the song was over. Kasria looked up into his eyes and stood on her tiptoes to whisper, "This is where you tell me your name, stranger."

He laughed, "If I tell you that all this will undoubtedly end and it's just beginning."

"It can't truly begin if we don't know each other. You won't know if this will end unless you try. Our wolves already know one another, now it's time for our mortal sides to learn."

He grinned despite the uneasiness taking root in the pit of his stomach the idea of trusting her, a stranger, despite his wolf's belief was difficult. He leaned down to her ear inhaling her unique smell of lilies and roses, "Lucian."

It took a few minutes for her to put the pieces together but given their wolves connection and that his likeness was well advertised in the city due to his status he couldn't really be surprised. "Oh. Lucian is it. It's nice to meet you. Do I call you Sire?" She giggled at the question which made his cooling demeanor crack into laughter as well.

"No. You of all people will never have to call me that. I am simply Lucian."

She traced a hand down his face as if memorizing the contours. As her finger went down his nose she flicked the end with a sly smile, "Boop."

He grinned and mimicked her movements. She stood on her tiptoes once more pressing her nose to his, breathing in his breath, he closed the distance between their mouths. Her taste sang through him. It was mere moments that felt like a lifetime but soon he had to separate from her just in order to fill his screaming lungs. She looked just as wrecked by the separation as him, her eyes half lidded, gone with desire.

He knew they had to stop, to return to the group and participate in the social moment. As the next song started, he twirled her around and swayed their bodies to the music. The time for talking would come but for now he wanted to keep her to himself for as long as possible.

sixteen

ULFUR

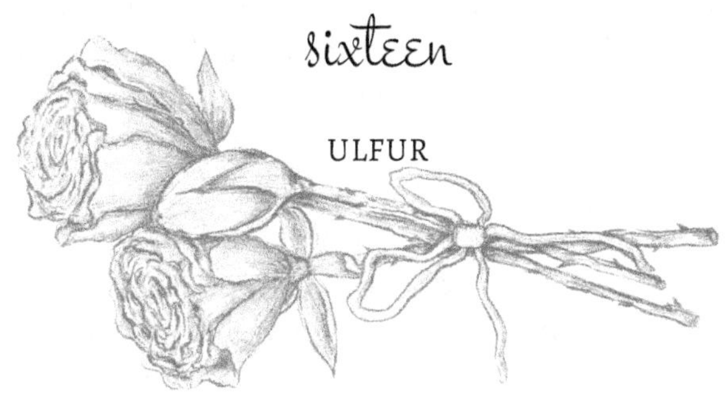

PALION - XITA - YEAR 7557

> Traditionally heirs to any Kingdom begin to learn the intricate details of ruling in their early teenage years. It is just another lesson by just another teacher from the temple. However once they reach the ages of sixteen and older they are expected to take on minor roles in governance, all with heavy oversight from the ruling monarch. It is rare that a blood related heir just becomes the ruler without a large amount of help on the offset, only in severe tragedy. On the off chance that a blood heir inherits without the lessons and guidance it speaks volumes on the ruling monarch before them.
>
> ~Palion Archives

The idea of spending time with Lucian and Zadon outside of work felt like a chore. However seeing the magic as his misguided prince found his soulbond was worth the awkwardness. In fact he was so distracted watching the socially awkward Prince, he failed to realize that his own wolf was reacting as well. Scanning the room his eyes landed on the curly haired blonde next to the object of Lucians affection. Automatically his mind began to catalogue the differences between the blonde and his best friend, the one he had yearned to belong with. He shut down the line of thinking as fast as he realized it was happening. He knew it wasn't productive, no matter how betrayed he felt by the Gods.

He had been so certain Suzu would be his soulbond the feelings of affection and acceptance having been built on since they were children. He knew he loved her the first day he met her.

At the age of ten, his constant companions had been other wolf pack children whose families lived and worked in the palace. A group of boys within that worked hard to perfect the art of pranking, both the other children and the adults. Ulfur had craved their acceptance despite the fact that they were a bit older than him. So when the day finally came that they sought him out and let him follow along while they orchestrated a prank on the Palace Governess, he was all too eager to do it. Even though he had no idea what they were actually doing.

Suzu had just moved to the palace, her father accepting an advisory role due to his supreme knowledge on some obscure shifter nonsense. Over the years Suzu had tried explaining the details to Ulfur, but his eyes merely glazed over due to all the technical jargon. The fateful day they met she had arrived at the learning wing just in time to see the Governess raising her arm to strike Ulfur's palms with a ruler. Ulfur could still see the Governess' face as she had unwrapped her prepared lunch only to find it smeared with horse dung. He hadn't done the smearing, but he had been the one delivering it and determined to earn respect with the pack he kept his mouth shut. Suzu stormed up to the Governess, full of a confidence that Ulfur continued to marvel at all these years later, placed herself in the way of the falling arm. The words she spoke next still lived in his memory as fresh as the day she had uttered them.

"If you were halfway decent at your job this boy wouldn't have fallen for the obvious lie he was fed by his so-called friends. My father will of course have to be notified if you choose to continue on this path." Then she had done the bravest thing for a ten-year-old slip of a girl, she had gestured with every ounce of disdain in her body to the ruler still resting in the Governess' hand.

Once the Governess had started breathing again, the shock having robbed her of the necessary air. She had stepped back fumbling with apologies and shoved at Ulfur's shoulder releasing him. Suzu had taken his hand quick as a snake yanking him behind her as she ran them to freedom a girlish giggle escaping her to dance upon the wind.

That had sealed the deal for him. He was gone for her, but the Gods apparently had other plans for his soulbond connection. He had avoided all other females until now and he couldn't really ignore his wolf's fascination with the blonde. Taking a deep breath he brushed against Lucian's wolven consciousness. *Invite her friend to the table please.*

Lucian's humor floated to him, and he watched with a detached excitement as the blonde followed her friend and his, her eyes locked on him. There wasn't an available chair which had him starting to stand but she laughed. "Oh no, you don't. You requested me to join you so now you get to be a chair."

He grinned at her his mind and soul seeming to connect back together. "You have to meet Suzu. My Gods she would love that sass." He slammed his mouth closed. *Don't bring up other girls when a pretty one is sitting on your lap.*

The girl on his lap wrapped an arm around his neck. "I bet she is a very interesting female. Perhaps you'll introduce us one day. In fact I think you should have brought her tonight."

Ulfur's heart skipped a beat as his mind wandered down some very sensual places; places that included red and blonde hair fanning out together on his bed. He shook his head, the dark pub and enclosed atmosphere must be messing with him. He leaned over whispering in her ear to ensure only she would hear him. "She will love you, but before I introduce you, I need a name."

She wiggled on his lap causing him to clench his jaw trying to avoid thinking those thoughts from just moments ago. She laughed as if she knew the power she had over him. "My name is Belvina Feo."

"Belvina." The name rolled off his tongue sounding so pleasing to his ears. He felt something shift inside, but his wolf remained quiet not claiming her as his mate despite clearly liking her. Inwardly he shrugged opting to focus on the moment in front of him. "Well beautiful Belvina can I get you a drink?"

Belvina grinned shaking her head coyly. "I would rather dance."

Ulfur dramatically groaned. "That is the one thing I am not talented at. Ten minutes into our epic adventure together and you've found my weakness."

Belvina laughed so hard she fell off his lap. Ulfur snagged her around the middle, just in time to keep her off the sticky floor. "Woah now. It's not that funny."

His pride took a backseat at the luminous quality of her smile as she gazed at him. "Come on you Big Lug let's dance. I'll even help."

His heart stuttered. *Big Lug* was the nickname Suzu had given him when he was a kid. She stood up and pulled at his arm not realizing something had stalled him, he smiled not letting his stunned moment halt their fun. She pulled him to the center of the dance floor nimbly dodging bodies. Ulfur had more difficulty dodging the bodies because of his broad shoulders but calm nods and half smiles assuaged hard feelings.

Belvina began shifting her body and Ulfur felt like it sent him into a trance. He stood stiff unsure how to move or where he was allowed to touch, her skirt swirling fascinatingly around her calves. She turned back around eyes on him the smile beckoning him forward. Yet before he could move, he watched a hand snake around her abdomen. A hand that was most decidedly not his.

He felt like he was stuck in mud unable to move quick enough. Her face fell from seductive smolder to confusion swiftly shifting to anger. His wolf halted him as he made to step forward to save her. *"Let her defend herself. Her wolf feels different."*

Ulfur was torn. He had been raised to protect. Particularly to protect women and children. Yet, he had also been taught to trust his wolfs instinct.

Belvina gripped the stranger's pinky finger pulling down hard on the delicate appendage, doing her best to make it meet the stranger's wrist. The stranger instantly doubled over, clearly she was strong and even without over exertion she was causing him immense pain. She led the doubled up stranger easily, forcing him to comply with a squeeze to the broken finger. At one point Ulfur was convinced the large man would wiggle free, but she adjusted her grip and broke another finger. Ulfur fell into step behind them as she led the man to Ulfur's empty seat causing the table, Juro and his paramour of the evening along with Zadon to fall silent as they took in the scene. The curvy Belvina shoved the man into the seat and leaned over menacingly as the stranger cowered against the tabletop.

"Consent is required for touching. Did I tell you to touch me? Did I give you indication that I was even remotely interested?" She waited clearly wanting an answer. The man however didn't move. "The answer you must be unable to speak because how dare a woman prove you to be wrong is... NO. I didn't give you permission for any of it. You are a pig and if I hear from anyone wolf or otherwise that you've put your hands let alone any other part of your anatomy on an unwilling participant I will hunt you down and gut you."

Ulfur stepped up behind her and menacingly added, "I will help her with all the resources I have behind me from the crown." He glanced at Juro and Zadon. Juro was nodding emphatically an arm banded around his female, but Zadon merely shrugged and inclined his head. He looked down at Belvina who still quivered with rage and was shocked when his wolf took over his vision a process that only happened when he shifted. Through his wolfs eyes he could see auras, and hers was glowing vibrantly. It glowed much brighter than any other wolf he had met except the Alpha. *Interesting. Yet another interesting, smart, powerful and gorgeous woman in his path, but not destined for him.* Why would the Gods keep sending women in his path who spoke to his soul but have their souls reserved for another.

He held his hand out pride at her for taking control of the situation radiating from him. She took his hand casually stepping away from the table without a backward glance at the sniveling pig of a man. She stepped into his embrace and looked up her expression guarded. "Why didn't you step in and take over?"

Ulfur shot a huge grin at her, hoping to comfort her. "You had it handled, and my wolf wanted to let you shine. He showed me just how brightly you shine Beauty. I am very impressed."

Belvina looked down shyly. "Not many male wolves would do that."

He leaned down to her ear. "Well they are idiots." He pressed his nose into the skin of her neck. Belvina began to sway back and forth forcing Ulfur to move with her. She smiled at him as he kept the moves going.

What a way for the night to change.

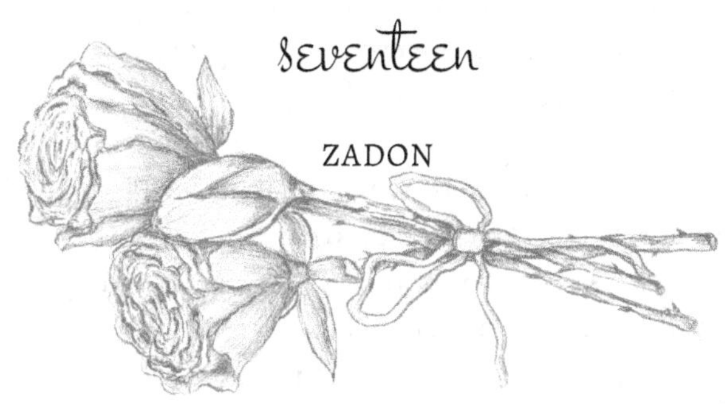

Seventeen

ZADON

PALION - XITA - YEAR 7557

Zadon stared unseeing out of the window in his rooms. A week had gone by since that fateful night in the pub and he had a rising suspicion that Lucian was battling the darkness the demon's blood had created. The newfound strength that the Alpha title gave him coupled with his supposed mate, giving him just enough power to keep the monsters at bay. Perhaps it was boredom, perhaps an internal instinct but he had to pull the evil side, he had nicknamed the Enforcer, out of Lucian more often to build its strength.

The pesky barmaid posed problems. The Gods decision to present the Prince his soulbond, now when he stood on the precipice of great change left an itch under Zadon's skin, he couldn't quite scratch.

Yet perhaps she could be used. She could be the leash that Zadon needed to ensure complete cooperation from Lucian no matter the setting. He tapped his chin considering the options. If he secured Kasria's compliance he need not worry over the Berrid unknown. He headed out of his rooms in search of Lucian, internally planning just the right move to encourage the Enforcer to emerge from the depths of Lucian's consciousness.

He found the Prince in the main hall surrounded by wolven shifters jockeying for positions in the court. Zadon found it rather hilarious to watch the masses beg when the position was far from secure even for the prince. Zadon knew Lucian was far from capable of providing much power or influence. Harold's hate for his son continued to remain potent at every interaction. It was clear to him that Lucian's illusion of power and clout, would only last as long as Harold found Lucian's new position as Alpha entertaining. If the Prince made one false move the illusion would shatter.

Unless... He halted near a column considering. Perhaps that illusion could become a reality.

As the ideas swirled, he stepped toward Lucian not letting the petty jealousy he felt gain any traction. Clearing his throat he waited for Lucian's green eyes to lock with him. He withheld the chuckle as the panic registered in Lucian's gaze. It was apparent that Lucian wanted Zadon to intercede and save him. Instead Zadon merely jerked his head toward the Council chambers making Lucian extricate himself. The Prince was slow about it but Zadon knew with enough training he could fix that flaw.

Zadon slowly monitored his own steps to enable him to fall behind his Prince. "Sire there is a meeting with the guards today to be updated on the investigations. After, we could perhaps visit the pub. I noticed a certain female seemed to catch your eye last week."

He swallowed his own laughter as Lucian's ears turned bright red. Mortal skins were so delightfully expressive.

"Do you think she's even going to be there?" Zadon could hear the vulnerability and concern that laced Lucian's voice.

He nodded a grin overtaking his face. *Such weak mortals.*

eighteen

LUCIAN

PALION - XITA - YEAR 7557

Living with a parent who hated him had Lucian second guessing every minute detail. The new responsibilities should have come with a sense of relief that he would indeed inherit one day. Instead he was left wondering when the other shoe would drop. After all Harold never gave anything without a cost.

Lucian had thrived on stories of how his father used to be when his mother lived. Naya would expound on stories of a kindly patient king who doted on his loved ones with luxurious gifts. Lucian had never met that man. Part of him was convinced it was a mythical legend that the servants had created to comfort the crying child he had been.

Lucian stood from his desk rolling his shoulders easing the tensed muscles. The days of beatings were behind him. An almost skip echoed through his step as he navigated the palace hallways, excitement filling him at seeing *her* again.

He knew what she was to him, and had from the moment they locked eyes. Still he lacked the confidence in his own skin enough to proclaim it out loud. Not yet anyway. He made his way toward the entrance, pleased to see that Zadon was waiting for him.

Similar to the first night he met her, the Pub crawled with people, still his wolf alerted in his mind. He could sense her. The voices around him faded as his entire focus channeled into laying eyes on Kasria. His feet began moving before his mind registered seeing her. In the back corner right next to the small stage where a woman was playing a lilting melody on a string guitar.

He stopped in front of her to the giggles and gasps of her friends, but he didn't care. She was here and she was his. Kasria looked up into his eyes, showing uncertainty mixed with joy.

"Hi, Kasria." It was awkward even Kasria blushed undoubtedly embarrassed that this was his continual opening line. Lucian mentally kicked himself. His wolf set about trying to soothe his fears. *"She's nervous as well. Keep trying. She was made for us, Lord Culgan meant for it."*

Lucian cleared his throat "Would you like another drink?" Inwardly he cringed. Where was Zadon when he needed his help? He always navigated social interactions so much easier than Lucian.

Kasria smiled and raised the glass clutched in her hand, it was still full of an amber liquid. Inwardly he groaned but he did his best to keep his smile on his face.

"Ah well. That's great I'll just go get myself some." His head dropped as he retreated toward the bar top, draping himself dramatically over it. "Where have you been Z? You could have saved me some embarrassment." He heard Zadon's dark chuckle as a glass was pressed into his arm, the cool condensation sending a chill through him. He dragged his upper body up resting his chin on his hand using the other to grab the goblet. He winced as the tart liquid hit his tongue.

"More of this wine? I thought we worked our way through it."
The wine oozed down his throat leaving grime coating his innards.

"You loved it so much that I just had to dig out some more from the cellars."

He could feel his wolf shrinking in his consciousness causing a whine to infiltrate his voice. "Why does it have such an odd sheen to it? Maybe it's a bad batch."

He watched an emotion flicker across Zadon's face before it was schooled. "No sire. I would never serve you expired goods. What's happened with the female?"

Lucian groaned as his brain replayed the interaction "I looked like an idiot. I know she's my soulbond. I can feel it! My wolf agrees but I cannot string a sentence together. For the Gods sake I asked if she needed a drink while she had one in her hand. All her friends laughed. I don't know how I managed to get her alone last time."

A darkness swamped his mind as he took another swig of the wine, grimacing as it once more coated his insides.

Zadon chuckled. "They laughed at the Crown Prince? That doesn't sound appropriate. If she's still your, soulbond, as you think she is, she needs to prove it. Wait her out. Make her come to you."

"What if someone touches what's mine?" A growl emanated from him as the wolf paced in the recesses of his mind.

"Now sire if she's truly your soulbond she wouldn't let that occur. Let's just sit here, nurse our drinks and see what happens." Zadon settled onto the stool next to him, his back toward the girl that consumed Lucian's mind.

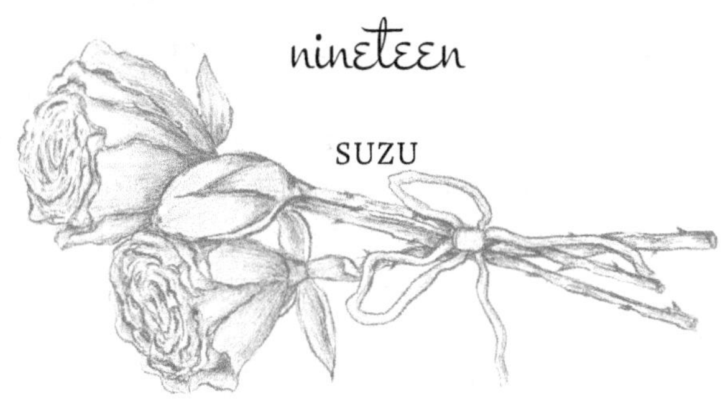

nineteen

SUZU

PALION - XITA - YEAR 7557

Suzu sat in the back corner of the pub watching carefully as Lucian nursed what appeared to be his wounded pride with Zadon at the bar. She didn't trust the demon, despite his full pardon from Harold and his obvious fondness of Lucian.

The hair on her arm rose as she stared at Zadon, noticing his eyes flash yellow before settling back into their dull brown. A man on the other side of Lucian stood seemingly of his own accord, moving rather mechanically toward the girls all centered around Kasria near where Suzu sat. Her breath caught and her stomach dropped as she looked at the man. His eyes were now as yellow as Zadon's had been moments ago. Something deeper was a foot but what could Zadon need with this random shifter? *What was she missing?*

The man in question approached Kasria, a well-known wolf female. Always the first to help and a favored candidate for the open Luna council seat, a swagger in his step. His eyes still an eerie yellow. Suzu tightened her grip on the mug in front of her, pulling the hood closed with the other hand. As much as she may want to step in it was vital to maintain discretion. Thankfully she was close enough that her superb hearing could just make out what was being said.

"Come on sweetheart. You should reward me, personally. After all, I was the man who saved those younglings." He lunged in grabbing her wrist in a clearly bruising grip.

Suzu watched intently, a blonde stood right behind Kasria waiting to step in at her signal while all the other women shied away from the large imposing man. Kasria stood strong despite his clawing grip on her wrist.

"Marug, you must be inebriated because this behavior is below you. You have earned yourself accolades with the pack, now unhand me before I take you down in front of the pub."

"Bah! A woman such as you take me down? Not possible." He pulled her closer using strength Suzu knew he didn't possess on his own, being only an omega. "You will give me what I want, wench."

This was whispered in Kasria's ear but echoed around Suzu's mind, her hearing making it sound like he shouted. Her fingers cramped around her glass with the effort it took to keep her seat. Kasria pulled her arm away, but it proved a feeble attempt compared to Marug's newfound strength.

Suzu had reached the end of her patience as he began dragging Kasria out the back door, the patrons of the pub scrambling away but not interceding. A roar split the air that had the pub silent as a pin. Only the wizened old drunk wolf singing off key in the corner was oblivious as Lucian stood.

Finally! Suzu expected his wolf to appear, to claim Kasria. The rumors of the two being soulbonds having flown ever since their first meeting. Yet it wasn't a wolf that greeted the pub, it was Lucian in his mortal form, then again somehow not quite. He was darker, in some way, more unhinged in his eyes than Suzu had ever seen him. As he rushed Marug his movements were not the smooth gliding of a wolf on the hunt instead they were jerky and disjointed as if his very muscles were repelling the orders.

The hair on Suzu's arms rose as Lucian spoke his voice now several octaves lower than before. "Hands off what's mine."

The man glowered but tightened his grip on Kasria's arm. She didn't seem to notice her attention focused wholly on Lucian. Lucian's fist snapped out faster than even Suzu could track. A loud crack resounding through the now quiet bar.

The man didn't move, not even to lift his arms to guard his own face. But it didn't stop Lucian from flinging his arms, flying so fast they blurred. It didn't take long for the man's grip to loosen and once she could Kasria stepped aside her hand raising to her mouth, shock, and disgust on her face.

The man crumpled to the ground, blood seeping from everything Lucian touched. Kasria stepped closer to him, her face a hardened mask. "Lucian. Stop."

The fists slowed becoming more jerky and mechanical all the same they still flew. Suzu gasped for breath not realizing she had even held it. Kasria reached forward her own motion slow and unsure as she gripped Lucian's arm just above his bloodied forearm.

"Lucian come back to me."

His fists stilled in midair and Kasria took this moment to pull his arm positioning him with his victim behind him.

"Lucian look at me."

Suzu watched in awe as Lucian came back into his body. A process she would have imagined impossible had she not seen it. Zadon walked up to the couple and Suzu would bet he was actively swallowing immense amounts of rage. His attention focusing on Kasria.

Kasria did not deign to look at the demon, instead

ordered. "Get rid of the body and bribe those who need it I shall see to the Prince."

Rage swarmed Zadon's expression. "You don't give me orders. You have no title."

Suzu gasped at the look on Kasria's face as she whirled on Zadon. "I am his Mate titled or not. A Mate to the Alpha holds power, demon. You will bow down or the wolves will answer the insult."

Every wolf in the pub stood arms crossed or chests puffed intimidatingly. Zadon's gaze flicked around the room before he took a measured breath. "I shall clean the Prince's mess."

He turned on his heel making his way to the pub's bar top.

Suzu nodded decisively, settling in, waiting for the pub to settle back into its normal rhythm. Her eyes snagged a few times on Kasria's blonde friend as she motivated the other ladies to help clean the pub. Soon enough Suzu felt it was safe to stand and slip out the door. Her head buzzing with information to filter to Harold.

twenty

LUCIAN

PALION - XITA - YEAR 7557

> Wolven politics can be rather simple when left to their own devices, away from the stressors of Royal life. There is one pack of wolves within Palion, known as the Palion pack. It is split, some wolves choosing to stay close to the Palace to ensure that wolf needs are heard while the rest dwell on the outskirts of the city. The pack is led by the Alpha and the Luna. While the Alpha post is ordained by the Gods, the Luna position is most often picked by the people. When you add the complications of Royalty into the pack dynamics things get messy.
>
> ~Culgan Temple Archives

It was like viewing the world through the bottom of a clear glass. Distorted and hazy. The noises muted and incomprehensible. The only thing keeping him sane in the moment was the scent of roses sharp in his nose and a golden aura in his mind shining around his wolf, forcing the darkness back.

A soft hand grasped his, leading to somewhere new. He could just make out her distinctive sound. A joyful chatter ringing through him like a bell. After a few minutes of faithfully following his rose scented mate, his nose picked up the familiar scent of the palace grounds. Misshapen blobs appeared more familiar the farther they walked.

Lucian tried to talk, to communicate the horror he felt, to show her the real him amidst the monster. Yet his body still struggled as if its basic motor functions worked but anything beyond that was too much. Somehow he could scent his own bathing chamber. They had made it. She continued talking to him, but he only understood every third word or so.

"...stool...sit...your...need...clean...first...you...communicate...It's...not..."

He felt the coldness reach his skin before his mind registered that she had stripped him down. She was caring for him in his most vulnerable state. Something unknown began to build in his chest, his heart swelled with emotions he had yet to experience.

"It's okay, no need for tears. Lucian. I suppose I can call you that now."

He frantically blinked as the furniture and shapes suddenly took sharp focus. He turned his head, his gaze meeting hers.

"Oh."

Desperate, he opened his mouth, but nothing came out. He slammed his eyes shut and hung his head in despair. He wanted nothing more in this moment than to communicate yet nothing was working properly.

"It's okay. I can feel you here." He looked up through his lashes and saw her point to her chest. "I can fill in the talking for now. I ramble a lot anyway, well except during official settings. Then I wear a rubber band and flick myself to keep the rambles quiet. You however, get to enjoy the full blown rambly mess."

He lifted his chin meeting her gaze, enjoying the blush that filled her face.

"Do you think you can finish up on your own?"

Panic filled his entire being at the thought of her leaving. She was quick to shake her head.

"No, no I'm not leaving but I thought you could have some privacy and I could get you some clean clothes. I'll keep talking and you'll still be able to hear me."

He took a deep breath and nodded slowly. She hesitated, staring at his eyes intently. She waited three heart beats before nodding.

"All right. It's real quick. Just do an all over scrub. Let's see, you need trousers and a shirt. This is quite the view Lucian. I bet in the daylight you could just make out the kingdom gates."

He blindly grabbed a bottle of soap as she continued talking. He was grateful because it reassured him that his hearing still worked. She was real and somehow she had banished the darkness. He could feel it at the back of his mind pushing against whatever magic she was using to block it out.

He dunked his body, as the water cut off her smell and sound, his mind floundered the golden aura dimming.

He opened his mouth on a silent scream as his consciousness tried to stand its ground against the taloned monster living in his head. Hands gripped at his arms squeezing painfully as they hoisted him up.

"I am here. Lucian. I am here. Still right here."

He shuddered as the tension melted from his bones, nodding his head, his upper body draped across the lip of the tub.

"Out you go Princeling. Come on." A fuzzy bath towel

draped across his back as he hunched over himself, the shivering starting to take hold. "Come along. The dry clothes are here. Then I will get you all tucked into bed. Perhaps you have a book around here and I can read to you."

Lucian silently complied, listening intently as she chattered about the girls she had been with at the pub. The sound reassuring, filling him with warmth even in his coldest moments. The clothes elicited a new feeling of shivering as the fabric activated his skin's nerve endings. Kasria didn't break her speech just shifted him to the bed. He laid on the too soft mattress, his eyes tracking Kasria. He tried again to speak his voice, finally deciding to work.

"Stay." It came out weaker than he wanted.

Kasria stopped talking, staring at him with her mouth open wide. "Uhhh. Yeah. Yes, I can stay."

He watched as she toed off her shoes and climbed into the bed. He groaned as he turned on his side, draping an arm around her middle pulling her into him. She sighed deeply and curled into him. She began to talk once more in a hushed tone.

"Once upon a time there was a great creature with wings so large they could blot out the sun..."

It took no time at all for him to lose consciousness. Yet, it wasn't a restful sleep. A wolf blacker than night waited for him.

"I am disappointed, Lucian. You were chosen as a bridge, the being to bring peace to the land shifters. Yet you're not helping those that are most in need. You need to save the ruling family of Drakore. Their family line is key to much that has yet to be revealed. I have made sure you have the one thing you need to fight the forces working against you here. Protect her. Protect them and build your world or it will cease to exist."

Shock filled him as his eyes jolted open breath coming in sharp pants. Kasria lay next to him, her brown hair splayed across his pillow. She moaned as she turned toward him. A shaft of moonlight draped across her face. A calm filled him at the sight. His heart rate normalizing. He tucked himself around her once more determined to do his best to keep her close and safe.

twenty-one

ULFUR

PALION - XITA - YEAR 7557

He shot up in the bed terror clutching at his sternum. Mentally he struggled to find out what had brought him jolting awake. It only took a few moments of internal reflection to hear his wolf's voice. *"Something is wrong with Belvina. Her wolf is in distress."*

That motivated him well enough to get his clothes thrown on and his ass out the door. "Where is she?" He mentally asked.

"She's in the pub or at least outside of it. Something big has happened the entire pack is uneasy, and we can't reach the Alpha."

Ulfur cursed. If his wolf couldn't reach the Alpha, then something had happened with Lucian. Yet what could it have been. They didn't have enemies with the Lykos family especially now that Kasria and Lucian were sniffing around one another. Not bothering to think it through anymore he welcomed his wolf, shifting fully and bounding out from the guard house, heading toward the pub.

He sniffed the air as he reached the stretch of road before the building in question. He could smell all manner of scents. Kasria's faint rose scent alongside a dark unfamiliar one led up the Palace Hill toward the castle. Belvina's scent of jasmine and honey mingled outside but it also had another scent mixed with it, one that had Ulfur peeling his lip back with concern, hints of rotting eggs.

His ears began to pick up sounds of a struggle. "Let me go. I didn't do anything! You were right there."

It was her voice. He would know it anywhere. His mind began to panic, he needed to find her. His wolf focused though, nose down the smell of jasmine getting stronger. Ulfur caught sight of the two bodies locked together, her clearly trying to extricate herself from the man who rested in shadow. The man however was very strong, making the little trick she had used a few weeks ago while dancing useless. He could tell she was panicking too much to think straight so he made a split-second decision.

He shifted to his mortal form and ran up to them. As soon as there was an opening where he could punch the attacker without endangering Belvina, he struck. The man's head snapped back and his arms immediately loosened angling to protect his own face from potential further damage. Belvina's sobs exploded out of her as she stumbled away from the attacker firmly placing Ulfur in front of her. He took that as permission to defend her without worrying she would get upset. He administered a few more precise punches aiming for the midriff and then one more to his skull knocking the man out cold. He leaned down, verifying the slime was just knocked out before turning toward Belvina.

A scan of her from head to toe showed that she was physically fine. He sagged in relief as he walked up to her and pulled her into a hug. "You okay Beauty?"

"How.. did.. you.. know?" She asked through hiccupping sobs.

He smiled into her hair as her arms came around him, returning the hug. "Your wolf reached out to mine. I will always help you if you're hurt or scared. Your wolf knew that on some level. Do you have somewhere safe to go?"

"I don't know." She took a shuddering breath before standing up and wiping under her eyes. "I just moved here from the country. Kasria was letting me stay with her, but she took Lucian back to the Palace. After what happened I don't think she will let him out of her sight."

Ulfur remembered that his wolf had claimed that no one could get in contact with the Alpha and wanted to grill her over what had happened however instead he draped an arm around her shoulders. "Do you need anything from inside? You're gonna stay with me. There's a guest room at the bunkhouse with your name on it. You'll be safe and you won't be alone until you're ready for sleep. You can tell me all about what happened."

Belvina glanced back at the slumped form of the attacker and shook her head a shudder working through her. "I don't have anything inside. Will he get in trouble?"

"Yes. I don't want you to worry about it though. I will handle it. I didn't get a chance to tell you when we first met but I am not merely a guard. I am the head of the guards, I make all the decisions." Ulfur gently directed her up the palace hill.

She gave him a small smile and allowed him to move her. As they walked, he listened as she described the odd situation around Lucian's most recent visit to the pub. He would need to discuss with Juro and conduct interviews, to see if they could narrow down what had actually triggered such a sharp personality change in the prince.

"Thank you for sharing that. Do you mind if I ask what happened in the alley?"

Belvina broke off their physical contact her energy feeling a bit wild. "I was inside verifying that the wolves in the pub were all agreed to back up Kasria. I may have been using some of my influence to manage it but that's beside the point. I must have gotten too in the zone with it because I didn't notice the man as he came up beside me. All I could see was his bright yellow eyes. He kept insisting that since she, being Kasria, had sanctioned Marug's death I would pay the price. I would take what she would have gotten from him. Honestly it made little sense, but he was insanely strong. I couldn't break free and as you know my wolf is formidable." She rubbed her arms unwilling to look at him. Throwing a shrug, she continued. "I am glad she managed to get you there though. I shudder to think what he wanted to do with me."

The thought of what could have happened had Ulfur's blood running cold. "You are enough Belvina. It's fine that you had a moment of weakness. I don't judge you for that. You understand that right? I know not everyone is safe to be yourself around but I am. You may not accept that yet but I will do my best to show you the longer we know one another."

Belvina looked at him then finally met his eye. "I was raised to be strong Ulfur. To be the strength of the country pack. Someday you may learn more about that, but I was sent as a potential candidate for the Luna position. Granted having met Kasria there is no chance I will compete with her, but I cannot be *weak*."

Ulfur grabbed her hand and kissed the top. "Come on let's go get you settled. Then I will show you that there is strength in moments that appear weak. It takes time and an open mind. Never fear."

twenty-two

HAROLD

PALION - OXI - YEAR 7557

Harold glared at the golden statue in the corner. His father had spent the exorbitant coin to get a looka-like bust of Culgan the God of the Wolves. As the kingdom dedicated to the sanctity of the land his father felt it was prudent to honor the God of the largest group of land shifters.

Harold found it ridiculous. The mangy dogs didn't need their own deity and that deity sure didn't need to be honored. *It's not like Culgan stepped in for his Queen in her hour of need, instead he let his wolf subject die.* It also certainly wasn't because his pitiful excuse for a son had been selected as Alpha. His thoughts were broken when the door slammed open and Suzu rushed forward, arms full of papers.

"We have a problem."

"I may have agreed to your appointment. I did not agree to your disrespect. Would you care to try again?" His mood darkened as she didn't even glance in his direction.

"Your son has become something truly unhinged."

Harold scoffed. "He's just a wolf Suzu. I know you've seen those before growing up in the Capital."

She finally met his eyes, a look of steely determination that he had never seen before resting on her face. "No. This wasn't his wolf. This was darker. It emerged when his soulbond was threatened."

All other words faded to a buzz filling Harold's head around that fated term. Images of his beloved Queen Larial filtered in through the buzzing. Her smiling face, so like Lucian that the pain swamped him. He didn't realize he had lost control until the tentative touch of Suzu at his shoulder jerked him back to his dark reality. The one where she did not exist. All because of their *son*.

Harold took several deep breaths forcing himself up, his neutral mask once more in place. "Who is she?" Damn his voice still shook with emotion.

Suzu retreated back to her side of the desk watching him warily. "Kasria Lykos, a long time favorite for the vacant Luna position. If my suspicion is correct, she will get it naturally. She claimed Lucian last week when he was overtaken by this evil nature."

"Who are her people?"

"The Lykos family have been strongly connected to the wolf clan for a century or more."

Harold thumped the desk. "What do they do Suzu? I won't have just anyone ruling this land. We saw that the Great Power works better with royals. He's already betrothed to a Princess."

Suzu rolled her eyes, but he waited her out tapping impatiently on the desk. He knew his beloved had not died due to her poor lineage. He had been brash in his youth and rushed to the throne not heeding his own parents warning that he should wait and try to find his soulbond first. If he had ascended the throne after marrying her, she would have had equal access to the Great Power, but instead his stupidity wrote the way for her death. He had taken the throne as soon as he was old enough, despite not knowing her and when they finally did meet, she couldn't be tied to the Great Power. She was kind about it, but he had always felt guilt.

Suzu cleared her throat. "I don't think that truly matters, Sire."

Harold interrupted her. "She's a bar wench. That pub at the base of Palace Hill is Lykos Pub. They own it, yes?" Her heavy sigh was all he needed. "Noted. It shall be dealt with."

"Hold on, Sire." The title was a ground out curse, but he let it slide looking at her once more.

"Yes?"

"We need her."

"Why in the name of the Pantheon would I need a bar wench?"

He watched her struggle to suppress her eyeroll. "She can control his internal corruption. She halted him mid attack and brought the Prince back using their connection. It's essential that she be brought into the fold."

He couldn't hold back his laughter. "Brought into the fold? Absolutely not. I don't need a bar maid to keep my son in line. Here's what we are going to do. Have my servant send for Ulfur."

He watched emotions flit across her face. Pleasure seeping through him as she merely nodded once and exited the room taking her notes with her. Females were really too sensitive to hold such important positions. He would need to begin the search for her replacement.

He didn't have long to wait before the burly man knocked at his study door.

"Come in."

Ulfur lumbered in standing at full attention, his entire

being stiff. Harold suppressed a chuckle; sometimes the title of King elicited some fascinating responses.

"Name and rank boy." He barked.

"Ulfur Hanklin, Beta of the Wolves and Head of the Guard, granted by his Highness Prince Lucian Ronnet."

Harold nodded along. "I have a mission for you. I am sending you alone into Drakore to warn them of the coming coup. While that is the main mission, I also insist you lay eyes on this younger princess. The older girl was quite the looker the last time I saw her likeness. I want to know why they would switch such a perfect match amidst the upheaval of their nation."

He counseled the young wolf until it was clear that Ulfur knew what to do and how to behave while in adversarial territory. Harold went so far as to walk Ulfur to the stables to ensure nothing would interfere with his plan. Now to deal with the bar wench.

twenty-three

SUZU

PALION - OXI - YEAR 7557

She waited in the shadows of the stable door for the King to leave. Her breath caught in her throat at the possibility that he would stand there until Ulfur rode away. Her mind eased as the noise of the King's boots turned away ringing out along the cobbled stone.

She silently stepped forward on her slippered feet. Ulfur grunted his surprise as she broke a twig under her foot.

"What are you doing here?"

"Aww Ulfur. Don't be like that." She danced her fingers up the sleeve of his shirt before gliding them off. He watched her fingers path, his eyes tracking every shift.

"Suzu. You have a tendency to appear when you need something, and I have somewhere I need to be. So if you could once again disappear that'd be great."

She giggled girlishly twirling a lock of her red hair around a finger leaning against him. "Ulfur, I don't disappear. I am right where I need to be at all times. I heard the King had a mission for you. I just want you to be safe."

She gasped involuntarily as he shifted position forcing her to step back invading her space. The smell of pine filling her nose swamping her senses. She scanned him head to toe before her eyes were trapped by his.

There was that all too familiar tug, almost a bond but something was still missing. Disappointment flooded in dousing the flames of desire that had begun to lick up her spine at his close proximity. Ulfur's large fingers gripped her chin preventing her from looking away. His eyes searched hers as their foreheads touched breaths mingling.

"We can't keep dancing this dance Suzu."

She let out a half-hearted chuckle closing her eyes as her logical side kicked in. There wasn't a dance and there could never be one. "Just be safe. He's sending you into a territory that merely puts up with our existence. You, my wolfish friend, can be rather blunt and I'd hate it if you incited a war or wound-up dead." She wrapped her arms up around his neck toying with his hair unable to stop herself. "I like whatever this odd dance is that we aren't dancing."

A low growl startled her, alarm bells ringing in her head before Ulfur's mouth was on hers, her mind unable to process what was truly happening. *It's him. He growled.*

The sensations flooded her causing her mind that never shut down to fizzle out short circuiting over the sparks coming from him. She moved on impulse pulling him closer, needing to be one with him. She opened her mouth to his questing tongue and moaned at the fresh mint flavor that flooded her. She barely registered that his hands were roving her body, nor that they had shifted a few steps back until her body made contact with the stable wall.

That contact jolted them out of the moment. She wasn't sure which one of them pulled back first but she leaned her head backward closing her eyes doing her best to steady her racing heart and thunderous breath. Ulfur chuckled darkly.

"Seems like we are dancing now, kitty cat."

She narrowed her eyes at him, the dreaded nickname bringing back a flood of memories. Her family had always been one of the few panther shifters in residence at the capital and the taunts still stung.

"Don't fuck up our relationship with the Berrids with your mangy dog behavior. I've worked too hard to..." She clammed up the blood draining from her face as she cursed the stupid hormones that had loosened her tongue.

He leaned in, nipping at her ear. "Working hard at what Kitten? What are you hiding behind those gorgeous sunrise eyes and many, many daggers you have strapped to you?"

"Nothing." she said it too fast. Lying to him suddenly seemed like a monumental feat when it came naturally with everyone else.

"No it's not nothing. But I'll torture you after I see this errand complete. Perhaps I'll seduce it out of you."

She stiffened at the idea, repulsion boiling inside her. Before she could snap back, he laughed sharply, striding away.

He called over his shoulder. "No. I already know that wouldn't work with you, but I bet if I withhold affection you'll crack before I do." He gathered the reins of his horse and walked it toward where she seethed. "After all, cats always need some love and affection eventually and as much as you may want to deny it, we aren't done yet."

Suzu had heard enough tamping down on the urge to cut him with one of the numerous blades strapped to her; she closed the distance a smirk plastered on her face. "Dogs are pack animals in need of companions. Plus interspecies soul-bonding doesn't end well just look at the throne. We are most decidedly done."

He grabbed her wrist before she could make her escape around him. He pulled her hand up to his face. She pulled half-heartedly but he met her gaze, a look of hurt mingled with seriousness echoing there. He kissed her knuckles and then licked her pulse point at her wrist sending her heart galloping once more. "I don't know Suzu. There's a deep tie between us that we have danced around for years. Don't rush to dismiss it or us." He whispered the words, but she heard them without difficulty.

"Ulfur. I..."

He shook his head once leaning in, kissing her lips, cutting off her denials and vaulted into the saddle. "When I return triumphant, we will find out why we are connected, and you will spill why my interactions with the Berrids of all people means so much to you."

She opened her mouth unsure if she would agree or argue but he was rushing his mount out of the stable without a second glance.

twenty-four

ULFUR

DRAKORE - OXI - YEAR 7557

> Shifters are rumored to be descended from Gods. Yet not all shifters choose to live in their shifter forms. Instead they opt to live their lives in their mortal forms. Another set of shifters only live in their shifted forms. It truly is up to the individual. Baelia accepts everyone's preference, no one group is held up above the others.
> ~ Tiva Temple Archives in Palion

Ulfur returned to his mortal form outside the courtyard of the Drakore Palace, inhaling deeply. It smelled of unease and a thick layer of discontent. Extremely different from what he had smelled on his trip through the celebrating city.

He strode with confidence to the main door knowing most of the guards were out at the citywide festival. He made it through the door and down the first corridor before someone found him. The room he was in seemed to be a random study, the bookcase holding odd books but nothing particularly interesting. He wasn't trained in spying, but he would do his best since he had the opportunity.

He was so busy his nose close to the books trying to smell if they had been handled recently when a voice broke his concentration. "Oh!" A female slight and willowy looking rather taken a back at his size stopped in the doorway arms full of linens.

He inhaled deeply letting his wolf sort through the scents determining that she was of the eagle clan. Her sharp eyes would have given him that knowledge though as he met her narrowed gaze. She dropped the linen on the floor just inside the door. "Who are you?"

He bowed at her keeping his hands clearly visible. "I am in need of the King and Queen."

She looked at him skeptically and he suspected if she had been taller, she would have looked down at him. "You may need their Highness', but no one gave you leave to wander the palace. I must request you follow me, I shall get you situated until they return."

Ulfur bowed low. "Of course Mistress. When will they return?"

She silently stepped to the side in the hallway an eyebrow raised waiting for him to join her. He did curious at how silent she would remain. She led him to the main entrance hall and then down a different hallway that led to what appeared to be the central throne room.

Ulfur took in the differences between the two palaces. The palace of his childhood had always been one made and decorated with light colors. Yet Drakore was its exact opposite in many ways. The palace itself was made with a gray stone, but all the draperies were dark and heavy. In some way it felt more regal and impressive than Palion's palace. *How did it occur that*

Palion feels more airy and open while Drakore feels more bulky and shrouded.

The throne room also held a surprise for him. The intricate thrones were not side by side as was traditional, even in Palion they had two thrones that sat next to one another despite only having a King. Here though it was a clear demonstration of who held the power in the relationship. He stood in the middle of the room waiting and the woman stood awkwardly to the side.

She cleared her throat. "I need you to tell me your name so I can announce you once they arrive."

He cocked an eyebrow. "I will tell them my name when they arrive. Don't worry. Now do you know how much longer it will be?"

Her brows scrunched and her arms crossed over her chest. "That is beyond my control. However, if you were to tell me your name then I could determine if I need to send a messenger to recall them faster."

He smiled. "I shall wait." He looked dramatically around noting there was nowhere to sit. His smile widened. "Should I borrow one of their chairs?" He gestured at the thrones at the head of the room.

The woman glowered. "You most certainly will not. I can tell by your demeanor and lack of propriety that you must be a dog from Palion. I shall have a maid deliver a chair and refreshments to you, but you will not move from that spot until she arrives, or I shall have the guards remove you from the palace."

He chuckled tucking his hands in his pocket. "The guards must be very good at hiding for I didn't see a sign of one on my way in. Never fear Mistress I shall wait right here for your return of a chair. Stay is the simplest command for a dog after all."

He swallowed his full belly laugh as she stomped away issuing commands to individuals he couldn't see from the open doorway. It didn't take too long for her to give him what may be the tiniest chair in existence. She smirked as he draped his thick limbs over it. He refused the water that had accompanied the chair on its own dainty table. He settled in to wait sure that the woman had notified her masters as was proper. He wouldn't be made to wait long, of that he was certain after all how often were emissaries sent between the two kingdoms without a deeper reason.

twenty-five

ZADON

PALION - OXI - YEAR 7557

Paying off the patrons had been an easy feat, getting Lucian alone again after his incident at the pub seemed nearly impossible. It had been a little over a week and the bar wench went everywhere Lucian did. The training yards, lessons, private meetings. If he was required, she came as well.

Kasria left the council room first and Lucian looked at Zadon avoiding his father's gaze. "Kas and I are going talk to her parents tomorrow and begin the process of planning a ceremony. You'll be a part of it right?"

"Of course, brother." Zadon internally groaned. He really didn't like the idea of that female bonding herself to Lucian.

Lucian grinned his mood brightening. He left the room, and Zadon was pretty sure he saw a skip in his step. Zadon gathered his notes and straightened his shoulders preparing to follow Lucian out. Harold cleared his throat interrupting his thoughts.

"Something needs to be done about that woman. She is not suitable for the throne."

Harold's words sank into Zadon's mind settling there for a few minutes before he turned realizing what the words actually meant. "Are you asking me to do what I think you are?" His demonic side roared to life in his mind.

Harold paced the room. "I will not administer a kill order. Yet if she disappeared, I wouldn't push too hard to investigate." He shrugged. "I think that Lucian should now oversee the dungeons. I will preemptively appoint you as the overseer in his stead, the spokesman for his court."

Zadon's greed crested in his mind. "Of course. Although you should expect his inquiry as to when you will allow him to ascend the throne. There is little else for him to oversee after that, at least internally. He has his soulbond, the palace and now the dungeon."

Harold glowered. "He will ascend upon my death. If he thinks that's all that it takes to rule a kingdom, then there is a lot more for him to learn."

Zadon bowed. "Of course, sire."

Mortals always gave more away than they realized.

Zadon headed down to the dungeon eager to lay claim to his own small slice of power. As he arrived the guards stiffened in his presence. Their natural mortal inclination to shirk away in fear due to his demon nature always caused ripples.

"I need the Captain of the dungeon guards to meet me in his office straight away."

The guard swallowed a bit put off by this order, not used to receiving them from Zadon. *They would get used to it sooner if they knew what was good for them.* He strode to the office in question and threw open the door looking around at his new little kingdom filled sparsely with furniture. He strode around the rickety desk already mentally filing away plans on upgrading the furniture. He managed to settle in the chair propping one foot up on the desk waiting.

The Captain strode in not bothering to knock scowl on his face. "What is going on here, demon? Why are you making yourself at home in my office?" The door slammed behind him.

Zadon blinked up at him slowly, his face a mask of neutrality. "Your office? As of ten minutes ago this office became mine." He ended the statement with a grin.

The Captain stumbled backward as the words hit home. "The King knows of this?"

Slowly Zadon pulled himself to a sitting position bringing his hands steepled in front of him. He sent magic down his arm to the topmost pointer finger allowing it to transform to its true shape of a demon's talon. "Yes. He was the one who declared it." Another finger took its normal shape. "You see King Harold, the wise ruler that he is, is preparing the next in line for his turn to rule."

A third finger popped into its talon form.

The Captain glanced down and gasped as a fourth finger turned. The man's eyes seemed glued down there as Zadon stood and strode around the desk. "Prince Lucian trusts me to mete out justice to those who have done our kingdom ill. I am also entrusted to guard those suspected of such crimes."

At this point he allowed his entire lower half to shift to its normal demon self. He relished the feeling of freedom it gave him.

The guard backed himself against the door staring in horror. "They would never choose filth such as you, especially if they saw you in your true skin. I'll remind them of just who you are. You won't get away with unlimited power. There will be a balance."

The rambling droned on, but Zadon ceased listening only hearing his own blood pumping fast in his ears. He fully shifted the sensation of rightness filling his mind. Wearing his mortal shell was very much akin to wearing an outfit two sizes too small. He turned his attention to the sniveling mortal in the corner rambling about justice and demons. The thirst for blood and screams surged within him. He needed to feel the hot moist liquid leave the Captain's body, to hear the snap of bones as his fist pummeled the life out of him.

His demon consciousness had been starved for far too long. He reached a long arm up his talons scraping against the metal armor. The screeching scratch jolted his brain out of the bloodlust fog. He took another step, reveling in the fear that seeped out of the man's pores. The acrid smell was momentarily overshadowed by a sweeter smell, piss. It ran down the Captain's quaking leg.

"Captain looks like you may need some help. Relieving oneself in the presence of others is frowned upon. Now that you see who you are working for perhaps you should rethink your stance."

The Captain spluttered his breath and heart rate erratic. Zadon took a deep inhale relishing in the scent of terror before looking the man in the eye. "Get out before I change my mind and make an example out of you instead."

The Captain scrambled to open the door, pushing his body forward but not close enough to actually touch Zadon his hands searching for the knob behind him. Before it opened Zadon issued his final blow. "Make sure everyone posted to my dungeons knows there is change coming. If they don't get in line they will be my lunch."

A squeak emerged from the mortal with a short jerk of his

head. Finally Zadon would be able to do things his way without kowtowing to the mortals.

twenty-six

HAROLD

PALION - OXI - YEAR 7557

Harold paced the study, anxious energy surging within him. He hoped Ulfur came back with useful news. A loud knock had him tempering his movements forcing himself to take a deep breath. Turning resolutely away from the door before bellowing, "Enter."

Loud boots crossed the threshold, the door clicking shut once more. "Report."

"To put it simply, Your Majesty the Berrids deserve what's coming. Whatever that is. They were rude and insulting. The only ones I feel bad for are the pups. At least the smallest one, she hasn't had a chance to do anything wrong."

"Did you see her? The youngest?"

"No. She is supposedly undergoing training at some other location. Cerial found her soulbond and they are choosing to honor the Gods choice over the previously laid plans."

"I see. Well then they are as lost of a cause as I suspected." An unhinged laughter bubbled within him. "It's fitting that my son attached himself to their movement." Shaking his head, dabbing the pinprick of tears away he added. "Everything he touches turns to ash."

Ulfur stiffened at that anger, beginning to radiate from him, impressing Harold with his restraint. "Is that all, sire?"

"Yes, dog. Off you go to your twice cursed master. Do give him my regards."

twenty-seven

LUCIAN

PALION - OXI - YEAR 7557

Another week had ticked by since the Gods warning. He had wrestled with how to help hoping that Ulfur would be enough. Yet when Ulfur returned mere days ago espousing how utterly useless the Berrid leaders were his thoughts were sent scrambling.

"How does Culgan expect me to get them to safety though?" He pulled his hair, frustration ramping.

Kas stroked his arm understanding radiating from her. "My love. The Gods decree it, so we must find the path that they can see. Who do we know capable of infiltrating the kingdom, or palace even? Most of our shifters stick out like sore thumbs against the reedy air shifters."

"But they want me to marry her! Part of me believes leaving them to their fate would be better for us." He gripped her hand needing to feel her and connect to her, proving that she had not disappeared. He watched as Kasria weighed his words.

"Who makes soulbond connections?"

Lucian blinked confusion over the divergent topic. "The Gods I suppose."

Kasria stood and began to pace the room. "Who asked you to warn and ultimately save the Drakore line?"

A deep sigh left his body. "The Gods."

She threw a glare at him. "Which means they know something we do not." Lucian rolled his eyes. She continued on with her words. "Who arranged the marriage with the Berrids?"

"My father." He couldn't resist another eye roll. He didn't believe in the Gods as strongly as most, especially after the fallout of his mother's death.

"The Gods will provide, besides what if you don't do anything and they die needlessly? You've heard the warnings my love. Your destiny is to help them."

Lucian rubbed his chin. "But who do I trust? Ulfur did get into the palace, but they didn't listen nor bother with him. I know because my father took great offense with it and now has decided he won't help any further."

Kasria walked up behind wrapping her arms around his neck, kissing under his ear. "Let's try my brother. Baryn is trustworthy but not beholden to your father. He also is a rather small wolf so unlikely to stick out."

Lucian leaned back into her embrace, getting distracted by her scent. "I'll meet with him."

Lucian was pleased that Baryn answered his summons promptly without question. Needing to keep the conversation private he held the meeting in his rooms even banishing Zadon from it. The circle was the tightest he could manage. He hated keeping Zadon in the dark but once it was successful he would read him in.

Baryn was as Kasria described a small wolf. Probably half the size of the average.

Kasria ran to her brother giving him a large hug. "Brother! How have you been?"

Baryn smiled shyly. "I'm good though I should be asking you that question. You've been gone for weeks." Lucian caught the glare sent his way. "It's almost as if you were kidnapped."

Lucian laughed. "More like she kidnapped me. One look and I have been enslaved to her green eyes ever since."

He enjoyed the flush on Kasria's face. She peeled herself from her brother, stepping into Lucian's side, giving his hand a squeeze. "Baryn. This is my soulbond, my Gods chosen. Lucian."

Baryn's eyes went wide as he stared at the two of them. "Truly? Your soulbond is the Alpha?"

Lucian laughed again. He found it endlessly hilarious when the wolves focused more on that title than the title of Prince. Kas shot him a *be quiet* look to which he winked and settled into the armchair waiting for the siblings to fully catch up.

Once it was clear the random stories and exclamations were drying up. He cleared his throat. "Baryn, we didn't just call you here to catch up. I need your help."

Baryn sat up straight, giving Lucian his entire attention. Kasria took her place next to Lucian perching on the arm of his chair, rubbing the back of his neck encouragingly. Lending him her strength.

"The Gods have issued me a decree. The family that rules Drakore needs to be saved. That is a tall order in any setting but during an active coup it may be impossible for one man. So the Gods have shifted their focus to the youngest daughter. Aurelia Berrid."

Kasria squeezed his neck gently bringing his word ramble

to an end. Baryn fell back into his chair his face contemplative. "If I can manage getting her out whats the plan?"

"The plan will be to protect her from whoever takes the throne. Then when we know more about the coup, we will give her the tools she needs to reclaim her throne." Kasria stated confidently. Inwardly Lucian chuckled, loving her complete disregard of his father's edict of betrothal.

"Ultimately you will leave and stay there until you can sneak her out. I don't want to hear from you until you make headway." Lucian directed.

"I shall leave straight away. Your secrets are safe with me. After all, we are now family." Baryn pulled Lucian into a hug. "Brother."

twenty-eight

ZADON

PALION - OXI - YEAR 7557

> There are some species that thrive with poly-bonds, the bonding of multiple souls into one. In places where that is more rare such as Palion it is seen as a great blessing when a polybond is found amongst the people. Even more blessings are seen when polybonds are created across species.
> ~ Tiva Temple Archives, Palion

He closed the peephole he had into Lucian's room thinking hard. This may be what he needed to get an edge with Tixdarr. A God led by mayhem. Zadon just needed to get his attention once more.

He double timed it out to the stable. Arriving with just enough time to lean lazily against the door jamb before Baryn appeared in the distance closing the space between them quickly.

Baryn met his eyes disgust flashing momentarily as he got closer. Zadon grinned. "Wolf."

"Demon." Baryn continued toward one of the easy-going horses.

Zadon followed closely behind. "I know the mission and I wanted to drop a few helpful ideas."

"The Prince said no one knows but those in that room. You won't trick me, Demon. I am not fooled by you."

Zadon laughed maniacally. "Believe what you want. However, in case you actually want to succeed, Dodsfell is touted as a dark and dangerous place. But that's just to keep mortals away from our stuff. The innocent are always welcomed and if you find yourself trapped taking your charge out of there it's always an option to use Dodsfell." Baryn turned and stared at him, mouth agape.

"You have got to be kidding me. Why would I believe you?" Baryn crossed his arms, his horse snuffling behind him.

Zadon's grin grew. "I am not surprised a smart dog such as yourself always has the answers. Each and every demon meets Tixdarr at one point in their life. It was made clear that any innocent seeking asylum would be allowed through the magic. Then they would be released out of Dodsfell by the Tixdarr temple. If you don't believe me then why are there holes in the wall within each kingdom."

Zadon shrugged and turned on his heel walking away knowing the seed of chaos would take root if the Drakore Kingdom was in as bad of a state as it seemed.

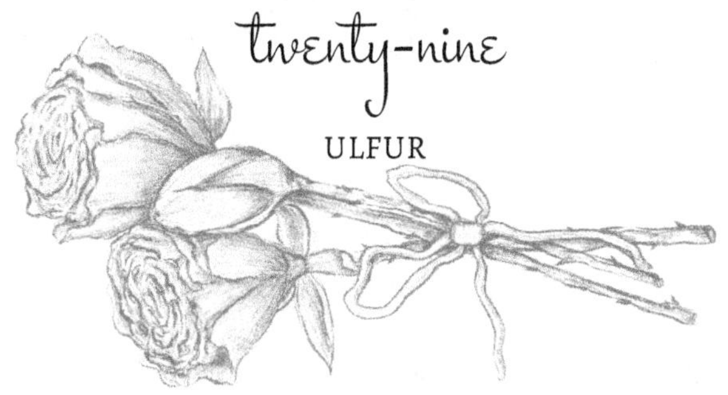

twenty-nine

ULFUR

PALION - OXI - YEAR 7557

The time in the training yard had gone well, the pups fresh from the country would be excellent additions to their force. Despite the productivity and physical exertion, his wolf wouldn't settle, pacing his mind hinting at something large happening. Yet he couldn't see anything out of place.

Ulfur headed back up to the palace intent on a shower and some food when his wolf interrupted. *"It's time."*

Time? He looked around again nothing was happening but up ahead he could hear the crisp steps of Suzu. He quickened his pace, they hadn't been alone since the stables, and he wanted to see how far he could push those feelings. A chuckle built up in his throat as she came into view her head down studying her papers. He had teased her about it in the past, but his studious little Kitten struggled to break away from the written word.

He watched in slow motion as she turned and ran straight into someone else. He stuck his fist in his mouth to keep the chuckle inside. He glanced beyond her and realized who it was that she had walked into. Belvina was giggling. "I am so sorry. My mother warned me, my clumsiness would get me into trouble."

His gaze darted between the only two women who had ever caused him to feel. His wolf howled in his mind. *"Mine."* An echoing click sounded within his psyche. Visions of Suzu in the stable, dancing with Belvina, his fantasy of red and blonde hair fanned out on his bed it all made sense. The Gods had sent him the women he needed, strong, stubborn and smart. He didn't know Belvina well, but his instincts screamed that she was exactly what they needed to be complete.

Suzu had sat up looking at Belvina, clearly not knowing that he was behind her. "Oh."

Belvina looked up and met his eyes before looking back down at Suzu, a bright smile filling her heart shape face. He realized as the light filled hallway glowed upon her that she had freckles that danced prominently across her face, her eyes sparkling in the sun. He found himself pulled in wanting to close the distance between the three of them his feet moving without his explicit permission. Suzu undoubtedly having heard him, glanced back behind her meeting his gaze, concern flitted through him at the panic and pain he saw settling on her face.

"Oh shit." she whispered it, but it could have been a shout with how loudly the words reached his ears.

Belvina looked between them all happiness and love shining out of her. "I knew it. You are here."

Ulfur smiled, it was clear that Belvina could feel the connection he did. What he couldn't understand was Suzu, she hastily stood brushing her skirts and not making eye contact. Desperate to stop her from running away he side-stepped placing himself in front of her. "What is happening?"

Belvina stood slower, studying Suzu and Ulfur. Her heart face falling, "I... we... both."

Panic grew in his chest clawing at his lungs and throat. "Both of you need to come with me, let's figure this out not run away." He couldn't stop the glare at Suzu who was actively attempting to back away and slink off into the background. He gestured both women in front of him, Suzu grumbled as she led them down the corridor and into a small study.

His heart hurt as Belvina's entire demeanor took on a sad and sullen tone where once there was happiness and wonder. The room Suzu had brought them too was currently being used as some sort of storage. There were chairs and tables stacked haphazardly against the wall. He took a step forward intent on explaining that he knew Belvina and to properly introduce them. Suzu interrupted holding a finger up imperiously.

He closed his eyes tightly refusing the urge to roll them. When the instinct receded, he opened them to see her crouching and studying the pile of furniture from all angles before going back to the door cracking it open to look to see if anyone lingered outside of it. "Alright we are safe to discuss this now."

He let out a heavy sigh. "I wanted to do this in a different way, however, Suzu this is Belvina. I met her back when Lucian met Kasria and I knew then that you two would get along. I didn't realize this would be the result though." He turned back to Belvina and gave her a warm welcoming smile. "She has had a rough time lately, but I think we can all say things are turning around."

Belvina smiled shyly. Suzu cleared her throat a blush on her face. *What could be in her mind causing that flush?* "I am sorry I ran into you. My full name is Suzu Zaral and if you need anything that Ulfur can't find feel free to seek me out."

She moved toward leaving, a feeling of pain and embarrassment filled him which didn't make sense. "Where are you going?"

Belvina stepped up her face confused as well. "You can't leave. We have to talk about this. We are bonded."

Suzu sighed heavily her back to the both of them. "I know you are bonded. Don't worry about it. You will have plenty of privacy in here and I'll make sure no one comes looking for Ulfur. Buy you some time."

Belvina's face scrunched, "You are bonded to us too Suzu. You can't leave."

Ulfur nodded stepping up beside her in solidarity. Still he felt disbelief and anger spiking. Suzu whirled around her finger out and her face explosive. At the moment it wasn't her face that caught his eye it was the paper in her arms. He scanned the document which appeared to be a weather report, but at the end there was a sign off that had the wheels in his brain turning. SM- Suzu.

Her propensity of being everywhere interesting events happened, she stayed near the library which held the Kings Study. She was supposed to be the head of various charities, ones he had never seen reports of. SM. *Could it be?* There had long been whispers that Harold had a secret spymaster. Vig and Suzu had been very close. He didn't even realize he was speaking until she held a dagger at his throat, the papers flying. "You're his spymaster."

The dagger was on his pulse point. It shouldn't be exciting, really it shouldn't. Yet, he couldn't stop the feelings. "Gonna cut me Kitten?"

"Oaths of silence now or you don't leave this Gods cursed room." Her attention was fully on him.

Belvina took two steps putting her hand on Suzu's knife wielding arm. "I meant both of you. We are a polybond." Her voice was sure and confident despite the fact that steel was on Ulfur's throat.

His wolf caressed his inner self. *"Polybonds used to be quite common and are seen as quite the blessing by the Gods. Since the pack moved to the city it has been seen less. Her wolf was told to come find us, she needs us just as much as we need her."* Ulfur cleared his throat, speaking slowly careful not to cause the blade to jostle. "My wolf has heard of this, the farther-reaching pack members support her statements Suzu."

Belvina tightened her grip on Suzu's arm, "We can't kill our mates. We need to support one another."

"I don't want to scare you Sparkles but I can prove to you we are not all mates. You and the Lug are undoubtedly bonded, but I am still very much alone. Watch." Ulfur groaned as she dug the tip of her dagger into his neck, he knew she wasn't trying to kill him. That would have been an easy task if she put her mind to it. He could feel her emotional turmoil roiling in her mind, a slight tremor in the blade all that outwardly displayed it. His eyes stayed on hers even as Belvina cried out in pain. A trickle of blood oozed down her neck mirroring where she had cut him.

"You're bleeding Kitten." Her smirk faltered.

"No. You are lying Ulfur. I won't drop the knife that easily, I was trained better than that."

He could feel his smile growing. It was just like his stubborn kitten to refuse to see the obvious. "Beauty do us all a favor and run your finger in the proof."

His mind was quickly figuring out that some of the foreign feelings had to be coming from his wayward kitten. As Belvina's finger traced up the dribble of blood a spike of heat came from the stubborn female. *Suzu, Suzu always running when things get complicated personally.* Belvina held up her finger and Suzu's eyes focused on the smear of red widening in surprise. He knew her and knew that she would need more proof.

He turned his attention to Belvina pulling her gaze to his. "Beauty what is it that you do? I have yet to ask you."

She smiled at him. "Well each time we see one another there are bigger things at play rather stealing the time away from small questions. I am a dress maker, or at least I hope to be. Kasria told me the palace may have a place for me. Which is what brought me here today."

He scanned her outfit. She was wearing a gorgeous pale blue gown cinched in at the waist with a smattering of daises applied to one hip and cascading down. All the flowers seemed to be hand stitched with beads and crystals. The top had long sleeves that flowed gorgeously, it all complementing her pale skin. "I will do my best to not damage this gorgeous creation you are wearing then." He pulled out a dagger from his belt and pricked her in the neck right above her collar bone. She scrunched her nose but didn't squeal or cry.

Ulfur watched Suzu carefully and noticed the flare of her nostrils as the pain hit her. Ulfur could feel the blood ooze down his neck, Suzu's eyes watching the dribble go down. Belvina's hand still gripped Suzu's forearm as she looked between the two of them. "Your turn Beauty, stab the stalwart spymaster. I don't think she will believe us until you do."

Belvina's eyes met his panic there. "I can't do that. I can't hurt her or you. You both are mine. I won't do it."

He internally cheered when Suzu turned to her finally lowering the dagger. "You need to. Complete the circle Sparkles." She held out the knife that had been at his throat hilt first. "It doesn't have to be at my neck, just cut my hand right across my palm."

Belvina's jaw took on a stubborn tilt and a fire lit inside. "You need to trust your mates." She took the knife and sliced quick. The red-hot burn roared across his hand as blood dripped from Suzu's. "I was sent here for you both. My mamma sought out an oracle when it became clear my soul-bond wasn't within our pack."

Ulfur glanced at his women pride growing at who the Gods had blessed him with. An eagerness spiked through him. "When can we get this bond recognized by Tiva so we can begin our life together. I don't want to wait to show you both off."

Suzu grabbed up her papers after re-sheathing her knife. "I will talk to Rusk and get you," she pointed at Belvina "a job with Mistress Tabbri. She needs an assistant these days especially because we will have a Queen soon. Tiva's main temple is in Drakore. Perhaps we can get the bond recognized a different way. We can all meet in the library tomorrow and I will have it all sorted then."

He grabbed her arm, pulling her into his chest. "You don't have to always do everything by yourself Kitten."

Belvina stepped up behind Suzu, close enough he could snag her with his other arm and pull her into his arms as well, jasmine and lavender mixing together in his nose. He kissed the top of both of their heads before releasing them. "I shall handle Rusk, Beauty shall handle the outfits, and you our strong spymaster shall figure out the recognition aspect."

He could feel her nod into his chest. He sighed deep contentment settling into his bones finally feeling as if he had found his home and purpose.

thirty

SUZU

PALION - OXI - YEAR 7557

Suzu had the hardest test of the trio, the ceremony, easily the most important part traditionally occurred in Tiva's official temple. This temple was located in Drakore and often there would be caravans of Palion people who traveled there once a month to make their dreams of soul-bond recognition true. Yet she knew there was a coup in the making there and she didn't want to put her mates or herself in danger. Her mind raced for an alternative. She paced the Great Hall trying to force her brain to work harder.

A statue caught her eye. A large golden wolf. She strode nearer, realizing that the wolf was that of Culgan, God of the Wolves.

"Oh."

She turned abruptly, forming the idea with every step. First she had to get a few key players to orchestrate her wild proposal and then tomorrow would be the best day of their lives.

I t had taken a lot of work over night to prepare the gardens. She had purchased extra manpower to create an archway of flowers big enough where the three of them could stand comfortably. The path from the library to the side door leading to their archway was lined with petals and flickering candles. Their faces were shocked as they followed her lead through the flowers toward the arch where two heavily robed figures stood waiting.

Her heart swelled as she turned to observe her mates' reactions. Ulfur was dressed in a mouthwatering suit of the finest cloth the color of the deepest blue, dark enough that in certain lights it looked like deep night. Belvina, her hair curled and pulled back quite becomingly wore a gown encompassing the pink and oranges of dawn. She fingered the skirt of her own gown feeling the prettiest she had ever felt in the gown of purples best seen at dusk. While it wasn't unheard of getting a soulbond recognized so quickly she was filled with fluttering butterflies all swirling in her chest. She barely knew Belvina, only trusting the feelings pouring out of Belvina's mind into her own. They both had the trust of the pack, but she felt like an outsider, being a panther among wolves. Ulfur smiled excitement radiating from him, Belvina's eyes were coated in unshed tears. Suzu gave them her own watery smile before beckoning them up to stand on either side of her as they faced the robed figures.

The robed figure in misty gray, wore an intricate headdress in the shape of a wolf head. The other figure was draped in soft green robes a light green veil covering their face. Suzu nodded to them in respect. She shot a look to each of her mates, grabbing both of their hands and squeezing tight. "I feel incredibly blessed to have been gifted not one but two soulbonds by the Gods. I want to celebrate, to do a huge party and invite all of our families. The logistics of that would have us postponed from honoring the bond for potentially months." Belvina opened her mouth to speak but Suzu shook her head quickly trying to get it all out in one go. "I know the wolves sometimes use Lord Culgan's Oba to solidify matings, so I took the liberty of securing her services, as well as having the Abbess from our small temple of Tiva." She shot a smirk at Ulfur. "I know the Big Lug here didn't want to wait, and I must agree life is going to be better when we are together rather than apart."

Ulfur pulled her in, kissing her hard cutting off the rest of her speech. "Kitten all you had to say was 'Marry me.'"

Belvina giggled. "He's right, you know. A giant party in the future sounds perfect."

A throat cleared behind Belvina and Suzu grinned. Shock rippled across Ulfur and Belvina's faces as they turned to see who was behind them.

It was Suzu's turn to giggle. "We couldn't do it completely alone. These things need witnesses after all."

Lucian and Kasria looked bashfully at them. "This would be my first wolf ceremony as Alpha. That is if you don't mind me witnessing?" Lucian grinned a bit.

Kasria spoke before Belvina had a chance, "If you would rather it stay private we completely understand." Lucian nodded along, pulling Kasria into his side kissing the top of her head.

Belvina squealed. "Kas!!"

Ulfur chuckled. "We would be honored."

They all stood in their assigned spots. Kasria and Lucian taking spots on the side, watching the three of them with wide smiles. Suzu stood in the middle with Belvina and Ulfur on either side. Oba Sarina from Lord Culgan's temple stood directly in front. The Abbess standing behind her.

Oba Sarina bowed to them, careful to keep the Wolf headdress on her head. "Lord Culgan delights in uniting the wolves of Baelia and while this mating is unique with the addition of a panther shifter, he was excited nonetheless." Oba Sarina blushed a bit, "I asked him what I should say to welcome a panther into this small pack. His reply made me laugh. Suzu Zaral is more of a wolf than even she would like to admit. In another life she would have been graced with an Alpha title and the power that comes with it. She cares for her people, her pack, more than herself." Ulfur began laughing while Belvina smiled at the flush that rose on Suzu's face.

Oba Sarina turned her attention to Ulfur. "Lord Culgan wanted to warn you, Ulfur Hanklin. You are a wolf driven by the need to save everyone. It's why you've been driven to be a warrior. However, he cautions you to choose who you save carefully. These two women need to become your first priority." Ulfur's gaze landed on first Suzu and then Belvina blowing them each a kiss.

"Yes, of course."

Oba Sarina nodded a grin on her face. "I didn't think you would mind. Now I come to Belvina Feo. Lord Culgan is quite proud of you." Belvina glowed with the praise. "You are a wolf far from home, yet you have thrived. His advice is to keep the ways of the rural wolves in your heart; they may come in handy in your future." Suzu's curiosity spiked but she waited. There would be a time for that after all, they had the rest of their lives to learn more about one another.

"Now for the technical aspect of this joining!" Oba Sarina clapped happily eliciting giggles as the headdress wobbled dramatically. She pulled a knife from her robes, an intricately jeweled one. "I need all of your hands held out in front of you please." They complied nervous energy crackling between them. "Now once the slices are bleeding, clasp hands until you form a circle."

Oba Sarina slashed first Ulfur moving quickly to Suzu the

cut swift. Suzu's eyes met and held Ulfur's as their bleeding palms joined, a sizzle of lust and power shooting up her arm from the point of contact. Oba Sarina moved to Suzu's right hand slashing just as quickly moving to Belvina's. Her head followed the Obas movements fastening on Belvina as the same shot of lust and power came up her arm. Suzu closed her eyes absorbing the feelings shooting around her body as the Oba closed their circle. She knew without having to watch when Belvina and Ulfur clasped hands. The magic growing in concentration. Their group was bathed in a glowing white light that was so bright she could see it through her closed lids. It tingled, a warm buzz filling her entire being, her soul feeling cleansed by the magic. She opened her eyes finally blinking at the bright light awe filling her at the sight of her family. Love surging within her mind through their completed connection, excitement on its heels. The sensation lasted mere minutes, but it felt like hours. As the light faded a new feeling took place in her head. It was a pulsing braid that felt strongly of love and safety. Her eyes widened as she could feel them in her mind, they were now their own little pack. They pulled each other into a group hug, joy and love soaring so high Suzu could have sworn she could touch the sky.

Ulfur grabbed her chin, tipping it up and planting a searing kiss on her. Belvina closed in behind her hands roaming Suzu's body, while she planted hot kisses on her neck causing hot and cold tingles to wrap through her body. She moaned against Ulfur's mouth, the feeling of her own dress suffocating her. She needed them both around her, over her, under her, touching her. A whistle broke their love-fueled moment.

"Now Lovebirds. Let's break that up before we need to erect some curtains for privacy. We have set up a house just down the lane for your celebratory night. I also had Rusk move you all into a much more luxurious apartment." Lucian winked at Suzu. "Big enough for Belvina to have a workshop and for Suzu and Ulfur to share an office." He smiled down on them, his arm curled around Kasria's waist.

Suzu curtsied low, filled with gratitude at their generosity. "We can't say thank you enough, Your Highness."

Kasria grinned. "We love you all and now you'll accept one more gift."

Belvina curled against Suzu's side excitement building "You've both honored us too much just by being here. We don't need more."

Kasria's grin grew. "This was an honor for us. Now accept the roles of advisors within our inner court and all will be settled."

Shock rippled through Suzu and her family. She knew instinctively that they would defer to her preference, due to their knowledge of her role with Harold. "Kasria we would love the opportunity to serve you both."

thirty-one

LUCIAN

PALION - TIX - YEAR 7557

Lucian read through the note again for the hundredth time. "What does this even mean? We are Drakore's neighbor! She's most decidedly not here." He pulled at his hair pacing the small office.

Zadon's deep voice penetrated the fog of panic, "That's not..."

"Look my love. Why don't we have this conversation alone." Kasria said softly. "After all it's a rather delicate topic."

Lucian met her gaze, the golden aura surrounding his wolf

brightening in his mind. He nodded agreeing. "You're right. Zadon my friend, I will have to meet up with you later." He turned to look at Zadon giving him a nod of gratitude as the man stood bowing with naught but a grimace.

"What would Baryn mean about neighbors?"

"Perhaps he secreted her away through a hole in their wall. She may be walking outside Drakore through the wilderness. You should send a small patrol through the neutral land closer to their border."

Lucian nodded absently. "The coup must have been extremely large for him to have to secret her away like that."

"That or she looks too much like her family. Blood can be telling."

"I suppose so. I wonder what horrors Rayner is bound to unleash."

He braced himself as Kasria neared. His darkness reared its ugly head, shoving hard wanting to bring to life the terrors he imagined. She lovingly caressed his cheek. "You will be okay, love. I will keep the monsters at bay."

Lucian nodded his world tunneling down to her gorgeous emerald eyes. His confidence in her ability to keep the monsters in his mind at bay soaring. He knew that he had to make the move now before something or someone interfered. "Kasria?" He kissed her temple and then her nose getting more lost in her eyes. "Karisa Lykos, please do me the honor of becoming my wife, honor our bond."

Kasria glowed, her eyes shining with tears. "Without doubt or question, nothing will keep me away."

He strode to his wardrobe and rifled in the deepest drawer to a small box Naya had slipped to him before she had been removed. Pulling it out he opened it his eyes catching on the opal and diamond ring nestled inside. The one possession that had been his mothers, it felt perfect that it would find its home on her finger. He returned and slid the ring on as he kissed her forehead. "My mother would have wanted this on your finger."

Kasria gasped staring down at the heirloom, tears forming in her eyes. "Lucian!"

A knock on the door broke the beautiful moment. Lucian ignored it pulling her closer and latching on to her mouth, hoping to drown in the taste of his one true love. The knock sounded again loud and insistent. Lucian groaned deeply, pulling away from her as Kasria giggled.

"What is it?" Lucian growled at the door.

"Urgent notice from the King."

Lucian grumbled as he strode to the door cracking it and sticking his hand out. The servant shoved a small paper into it. Lucian slammed the door shut again before unfolding the note.

Take your warrior band and protect the border. Disgusting vagabonds are being reported near the gate.

Lucian wordlessly handed the note to Kasria, shock radiating through him.

She hummed low in her throat. "Baryn might be right, the coup appears to be much larger than we all assumed."

Lucian nodded "I'm glad it didn't happen here."

Kasria turned to him urgently "But love, it could have been us. We aren't immune. Let's help these people. Don't hurt them."

Lucian gnawed on his lip considering. "If we do this, we are going directly against my father's wishes. This will be adding oil to a volatile situation."

"I know that but after our bonding we will be on our way to inheriting this kingdom. We need to start showing the people how we will act."

Lucian smiled tentatively. "You are a genius, my fantastic wife to be." He pulled her into his arms swinging her around in a circle as she giggled.

thirty-two

ZADON

PALION - TIX - YEAR 7557

> Zadon Duvlak the demon of Palion. There are those who whisper behind closed doors that he steals those who vocally dissent against the crown, more specifically those who dissent against Lucian. While it is unclear as to why he has dedicated so much time and energy to one who he has only known for a relatively short time, the truth is the world whispers of his dark deeds. He kills and tortures ending the lives of the innocent, yet he does so without leaving any sign of his involvement. It is whispered Tixdarr is helping him.
>
> ~Suzu's Spymaster Notes

Zadon stared his mouth hanging open. "You have to be kidding me."

"No. I need you to head up intake of refugees. Stand

guard near the entrance, to verify that the ones we let in don't have any ties to Rayner. We don't need him coming here trying to overthrow our kingdom next."

Zadon slammed his mouth closed, his jaw tightening. "Yes, sire." He saw a gleam of satisfaction in Kasria's eyes causing his muscles to tense further.

Lucian broke the staring contest. "We will be out there as well Z. I just need you stationed near the gate using that heightened demon sense to root out the bad eggs."

Zadon sighed heavily. Internally grousing to his best friend. *She wants me as far from you as possible.* It was clear since Kasria arrived she had done everything in her power to separate them.

Zadon bowed deeply, swallowing his arguments as he walked away from Lucian's study.

<hr>

It was monotonous work. Stationed next to the palace gate for hours watching air shifters trudge through. He couldn't believe the audacity of Kasria ordering him around or using Lucian to further her aims. He would figure out how to deal with her ilk soon enough.

He scanned the ragged bunch of peasants filtering through the gates of Palion. Boredom dulling his senses. No one here could actually threaten him; they were women, children and elderly and as such it mattered not to him who they let in.

A flicker of awareness surged within his mind. Someone was hiding something in front of him, perhaps several some-ones. He raised his fist causing the guards nearest the gate to halt the traffic of the mortals.

He walked through them smelling deeply. Mortals had a very distinct smell, much like sickly sweet fruit. Nauseating at the best of times. These mortals however also had the unfortunate side effect of being unwashed. The smell combination almost worked. He wandered down the rows of humans, varying ages all shying away from him as he neared. As he worked his way down the fourth row, it became clear that his target was one female. The smell had almost distracted him from her. Everyone cowered except her. She stood at almost six feet tall rather plain in her mortal shell but her smell, that of sulfur shouted her ethnicity.

Demon.

"Well hello. What do we have here?"

She stared silently, her eyes a deep dark blue, almost violet. She raised an eyebrow in silent question refusing to answer.

"Follow me milady." He waved the guards on sparing a halfhearted glance at the cowering mortals. He could have sworn an old lady winked at him. He shook his head as he led the mystery woman to the guard house just inside the kingdom. One lone guard sat enjoying a reprieve from the hot sun.

"Out."

The guard blanched standing slowly, "But. You can't, she's a lady."

Zadon started laughing. The lady stood to the side, unfazed waiting to see what happened. "She's far from a lady, boy. Go take my spot, we will be out soon."

The guard walked closer to the woman, his voice low but still audible to Zadon's impressive hearing.

"Milady, are you in danger? Do you wish to be here?"

Zadon raised his eyebrow, at her assessing gaze. The twisted side of him hoped she conned this mortal into coming to her rescue. He would revel at the opportunity for some fresh blood. Zadon leaned his back against the far wall waiting.

"I'm fine sir. Truly all is well." Her voice was velvet wrapped steel, soft but no less deadly.

The guard nodded once, throwing a glare at Zadon. "If you need anything you have but to shout."

Zadon snorted loudly.

Once the guard left, undoubtedly standing against the door listening through the wood, the woman found a seat crossing her ankles, hands folded in her lap.

"How are you here?"

"Same as you, I suppose. Shoved through the barrier."

Zadon raised an eyebrow "The barrier?"

"Yes."

"What do you want with Palion?"

"It's the closest kingdom to the gate."

"You know," Zadon stepped closer to his newest toy. "When I was shoved through the gate I was done so with dishonor, beaten to within an inch of my life. Yet, you don't have a scratch on you."

She smiled a predatory gleam in her eye. "I am clanless, the Lord we serve opted to send me through. I was such a *good* girl he did so without marring me. Apparently not all are that lucky."

Zadon clucked his tongue considering. *Tixdarr released her?* She may just be the way back to Dodsfell. "For now you shall stay as my guest. I'll introduce you to the other ladies and then perhaps you can explain how you of all beings earned *his* direct attention."

She stood a twinkle in her eye. "You have to earn that knowledge."

"I'm Zadon Dulvak. What shall we call you?"

"Valri."

"We need to get one thing straight. If I am going to allow you into this kingdom you will owe me a boon. One that I will call in whenever I see fit." Ideas on just how he could utilize a morally corrupt demon such as himself filled his brain. After all if she really was a clanless demon she would jump at the opportunity to join with him.

She studied him carefully. He was fairly certain it would

take more manipulation before she agreed, but surprisingly she nodded. He held out his hand to aid her in standing. She stared at it a second too long before delicately placing her hand on top of his. It wasn't lost on him that she didn't actually lean on him or need his assistance. He had no doubt this female would keep him guessing.

thirty-three

SUZU

PALION - TIX - YEAR 7557

Suzu blinked at the paper clasped in her hand. An official request for service by Kasria. The first of its kind, all in the name of helping the Drakorian refugees. Suzu had watched as Kasria's influence grew within the palace and she delighted at the results. Harold stewed over her lack of prospects and Zadon suffered from a growing ire that he was unable to truly unleash.

She wandered over to the seamstress quarters resting against the door jamb watching eagerly for sight of her beloved. Belvina came into view juggling bolts of fabric and Suzu stayed rooted to the spot marveling at Sparkles work ethic. She kept going, wholly focused even though she undoubtedly knew Suzu was there.

"Mistress Tabbri, can I borrow Belvina please?"

Mistress Tabbri sent Suzu a warm smile. "Who am I to stand between bonded mates? Belvina come here dove, your mate has come to fetch you."

Suzu felt Belvina's burst of joy and love along their bond. "Oh hello."

Suzu grinned, gesturing for them to step into the hall. Once safely there she pulled her into a warm hug, whispering into her neck. "Belvina darling, we have been summoned to help Kasria. She created a welcoming group for the refugees from Drakore."

Belvina grinned, wrapping her arms around Suzu's neck, kissing her cheek. Suzu's body lit up small fireworks erupting under skin. Belvina's hand traced down her neck leaving a trail of sparks until they held hands. Suzu gave it a squeeze.

S he led Belvina through the streets until she saw the large tents set up on the Palion side of the Kingdom gates. Suzu weaved her way through the crowds, her hand still clasped around Belvinas.

Once they reached the largest tent Suzu could just make out Kasria's brunette hair. "Come along Sparkles. Let's see how the future Luna needs help."

Belvina grinned. "I can't believe I haven't seen her since we were mated!"

Kasria was calmly directing various individuals with supplies for the influx of new residents. "You made it!! I asked around and heard great things concerning your charity work around the palace, so I just knew we needed to make this happen." Kasria pulled first Suzu and then Belvina in a bone squeezing hug.

"Thank you for including us!"

Kasria smiled broadly. "I'm hoping we can see more of each other soon. We girls have to stick together in the sea of testosterone that is the Palace." She winked at them both before adding, "I'll put you Suzu in charge of food distribution, each approved family gets a presorted box of dry goods. Belvina, do you mind helping my small group hand out clothes to those who may need them. It won't be perfect fits, but it'll be nice to give them something new and warm, some of these people are in naught but rags."

Suzu gave Belvina's hand a last squeeze before heading to a table surrounded by big boxes. She assessed the count and waited eagerly to get a feel for those fleeing Drakore. Perhaps it would illuminate what else Palion could do to aid those who remained in the coup torn kingdom.

It took a few hours and every muscle she had complained from heaving boxes, but her heart felt a bit lighter. She was even minorly impressed with Zadon who had seemingly adopted one of the refugees following her around like a lost puppy until Kasria separated them and had the girl handing out water. Zadon eventually growled and wandered back to his initial post at the gate, but they could all feel his eyes on his lady friend.

She was proud of Lucian and Kasria, setting up this situation for the disenfranchised. Belvina appeared to be enjoying her reunion with Kasria and the other female wolves, the bond between her and Belvina was alight with humor and joy.

From what she could understand most of the fleeing families were from the upper elite sent directly by Drakore's own inner circle afraid of what was coming, yet they had waited too long. Now the situation had turned dire, the Queen and King dead. The girls missing and presumed dead. Any mention of the Berrid family led to imprisonment.

thirty-four

LUCIAN

PALION - TIX - YEAR 7557

A knock sounded on their quarters that had Kas sitting up excitedly. Lucian looked at the door confusion marring his features as she bounded up. "Baryn!"

Lucian barely caught the man's face before she engulfed the smaller man in a hug. "Once your sister is done strangling you, come sit! Tell us what has happened. Where is she?" Lucian poured hefty drinks for each of them and waited impatiently.

The first thing that he noticed was the hesitancy. Baryn moved slowly, his eyes glued to the ground. Kas wrapped an arm around his waist, her voice low and full of love. "It's okay B. Just tell us so we can find a solution."

Lucian's pulse skyrocketed as Baryn took a deep breath. "I spent the first few weeks there scoping out the area. I also issued another formal warning to her parents, yet they did not heed my advice. I found her in the stables shortly after that and I should have stolen her right then but instead I warned her to run. As you know by now a coup has successfully taken

167

place in Drakore. Rayner Svenston is the ringleader, and I can assume the new king, but I didn't stick around to verify. I forced my way into the palace and since I had her smell from the stable, I found her easily enough. She's a spitfire but she's also tiny. She would not have survived if not for my help."

Lucian exhaled. The mission was successful; she was out of Svenston's hands. Kasria squeezed his arm preparing him for the next words.

"There were too many soldiers. Everywhere we went another group was there with orders to seize her."

"Could you not disguise her?" Kas whispered.

"I found her mother on my way into the palace. She is her mother's twin in facial features. There is no disguising that bloodline."

"So how did you get her out? You did, didn't you?"

Baryn met his gaze briefly, apology and sorrow shining out. "I was told if I got overrun to send her to an unlikely place, that there she will find aid and be returned."

Lucian stood abruptly pacing, his mind overwhelmed. "Where?"

"Dodsfell." Lucian's blood ran cold.

A gasp left Kasria. "Baryn, you didn't? An innocent sixteen year old released into a land teeming with demons."

Baryn slammed his fist on the end table causing the glasses to jump. "A high-ranking member of this court claimed it would be safe, so I thought if I got her into Dodsfell while we were in Drakore, she would be released at the temple. Only she wasn't."

Kasria took a shaky breath, tears forming in her eyes.

"Zadon told you?" Lucian's voice darkened. *What would Zadon be up to with sending a child to the land of demons and death?*

"Yes, after I left here, he cornered me."

Kasria nodded. "Alright we will just have to watch out for

her. Set a patrol along the wall and around the temple. If the realm releases her we will find her and help her heal."

Baryn nodded glumly. "I owe her a life debt for this mistake. I won't forget even if it's just me patrolling."

Lucian shook his head. "No. The kingdom owes her. Zadon spoke with misappropriated authority and anything she experiences falls on all our shoulders. I will see this put right."

Kasria smiled through her tears nodding along.

thirty-five

HAROLD

PALION - DRAK - YEAR 7558

"Who the fuck does he think he is?!" He couldn't cap the emotions despite seeing Suzu stiffen with his outburst.

"She's just trying to fix what is obviously broken. Drakore is suffering. Kasria…"

"NO. You will not say that whores name. She used her feminine wiles to get into the palace and I won't see it continue." He breathed deep, releasing as much as he could of the built-up emotions. "Send for my son and only my son."

Suzu stood leaving quickly and for once he was grateful for her silence. Unfortunately Lucian seemingly appeared mere minutes later, leaving Harold still struggling to rein in his temper.

"Sit."

Lucian growled a bit but sat readily enough.

"Your little slut has run her course. It's time to put her in her place. Since you are not man enough to do so it has come down to me once more. I cannot fathom how she swayed your good sense into wasting our resources for people who are not our own." Harold slammed his fist into his desk with enough force to dent the wood with his fervor.

"She's not a slut. She's my fucking soulbond and the future Queen of this kingdom." Lucian surged to his feet, body heaving.

"What are you going to do about it, son? Gonna fight me? Have you forgotten what happens when you stand against me?"

Harold dug into his power the long dormant well attached to the land. He awakened the wood floors urging the branches to grow despite the length of time it had been since the plank had felt the pulse of life as a tree. The branches began to wrap around Lucian's feet and ankles. Satisfaction swirled within him as Lucian's face blanched. "That's right boy. Remember the pain I am capable of. My resources are for Palion people not Drakore castoffs. You will cease this nonsense at once!" Lucian growled, pulling at the bonds that held him. "You will dismiss your two-bit whore and marry the princess I have secured for you. Or you will simply not inherit. Is she worth the throne?"

Harold could have cawed in satisfaction as Lucian remained silent. "That's what I thought!" He snapped his fingers releasing the wood holding him. "Get out and clean up your own fucking mess."

thirty-six

LUCIAN

PALION - DRAK - YEAR 7558

> Traditional Tixdarr ceremonies are overseen by upper-level Acolytes, unless it is a royal death. Royalty is the only exception, and they are overseen by the Oba Kana. The ceremony itself is rather straightforward. The body of the deceased is wrapped in linen and put on a pedestal in the place of honor while the overseer of the ceremony speaks about the ideas of death. The families are to remain silent letting the soul choose for itself where it will go next. At the end there is a moment of time that the family is permitted a final farewell. Once completed the body is taken to the Dodsfell gate and left against the magic which absorbs it through the barrier. Tixdarr taking a small amount of that individual's power as payment for the privilege.
> ~Tixdarr Temple Archives

. . .

"Lucian darling, are you here?" Kasria's joy filled voice echoed off the walls.

Her voice began to lift the darkness that clouded in around him. "Yes."

"Why are there no tapers lit?"

"Dark is better after today."

She came into view in his small sitting area holding a guttering candle, the glow throwing sharp angles on her face. Her face drew in, closing off the joy that had been in her voice. "What has happened?"

"My father."

He watched her approach slowly. "What happened, Lucian?"

"It's over. He has clearly declared that I am to get nothing. No throne or no you. My entire life's purpose has gone down the drain because we tried to help the less fortunate from Drakore." He dropped his head back staring at the ceiling refusing to watch as the words struck home.

"Wanna know something special?"

"Hmm"

"I met a host of amazing people yesterday. All of whom welcomed me without question." He felt her kneel in front of his chair. "They never questioned who I am to you or why we would help. They just wanted to be a part of this journey."

"That's great love." He couldn't muster up the emotional conviction to back his words.

She tsked impatiently. "You're not understanding love. That means he is but one man. One overly powered man. We can overcome that and keep your throne."

He tilted his head down finally meeting her gaze. "That's a tall ask. He wields the great power Kasria. He also cannot be reasoned with."

"What we need is more people on our team. I got to watch Suzu and Ulfur work, it makes sense why they mated Belvina, they all complete each other. Let them help us. Plus there's always the demon. He even seemed to have found his own friend. She could join as well."

Lucian marveled at the spark of determination that dwelled in her eyes. "I don't understand what I did to deserve you." He pulled her up into his lap snuggling into her neck. "What if I want to walk away from all of this. Will you come with me?"

Kasria's fingers pulled his chin urging his head up to meet her gaze. "Absolutely. Wherever you are I will be right next to you."

Lucian smiled. He opened his mouth preparing to proclaim his true love when there was a banging knock on the door. "Ignore it, love. The day has been long enough."

The door sounds continued quicker and harder. "Lucian, I know you're in there."

Lucian groaned in Kasria's ear. "I'll take care of it."

He walked toward the door gathering his nerve for what he wanted to do next; he couldn't have anyone accompanying them. Let his father take it up with the Gods after the fact.

He cracked the door, unable to hide his smile as he took in his lanky friend. "Hey Z. What's happening?"

"Brother! It feels like it's been ages since we've been on the town. Come let's catch up over a pint."

The darkness began roiling inside him, eager at the prospect. A small hand slid under his shirt caressing his lower back immediately calming the roiling shadows. Zadon's eager face fell at the sight of Kas emerging from behind him. It hurt Lucian's heart to know his best friend and his soulbond didn't get along.

"Sorry brother. I have plans tonight but tomorrow I want to speak about the creation of our own court."

Warmth and love filtered through the bond he shared with Kasria.

"Lucian, go with your friend. I've monopolized a lot of your time. It's okay." Panic bubbled up inside at the idea of leaving Kasria alone after the fit his father had.

Despite the surprise and hope on Zadon's face, Lucian shook his head. "Love, we have something we must do tonight."

Curiosity filtered into his mind, but he was grateful she didn't press. He needed them to keep their next task completely between the two of them.

Zadon nodded slowly. "I understand sire."

Lucian cringed at the formality but as he went to correct him Zadon had all but run away, clearly hurt. "I'll have to make it up to him."

Kasria giggled behind him. "Oh, most decidedly. But perhaps the girl he latched onto at the gate will provide him some entertainment." She pulled on his arm, tugging him back into the room. "Where are we going?"

"It's a surprise."

"Lucian! How will I know what to wear if I don't know where we are going?" His face split into the first true smile in hours as he took in her pouting face and crossed arms.

"My darling. Just wear something that makes you feel at your prettiest." He moved to his wardrobe grabbing an embroidered jacket and his decorative sword sheath, switching it from the plain one.

Kasria studied him, a smile unfolding. "Oh Lucian. Give me but a moment."

He smiled into the looking glass. After today the world would finally begin to go his way.

thirty-seven

ZADON

PALION - DRAK - YEAR 7558

He paced most of the night. How dare she control Lucian so? She enticed him, luring him with her voluptuous body. Yet how best to get her alone. She needed to pay. It would need to involve Lucian.

In the morning his mood had not changed much, determination threading through him to get Kasria alone. Lucian had tried to appease him. They had a group breakfast which for reasons he hadn't understood included Suzu and her lovers. Kasria had chattered happily, and the girls had filled in the tense silence, but it didn't calm his anger.

It took a week before the perfect opportunity arrived. Lucian was called to attend an issue in the tent city that had been created along the edge of the capitol. He had requested that Zadon come along but he had begged off, sending Ulfur in his stead.

Zadon pulled out a carefully curated note.

URGENT
A FIGHT HAS BROKEN OUT AT THE REFUGEE
CAMP. LUCIAN WAS INJURED. HE'S ASKING FOR YOU.
I'LL MEET YOU AT THE MED WING.
~ZADON

The bribes were already in place with guards who normally were stationed in the dungeon. Now they would line his route in and out of the med wing ensuring he would go undisturbed. All to orchestrate just a few precious minutes alone with her to be able to get her to the next place.

He sent a runner with the note. She should still be in the palace so it wouldn't take long to get her to show up. He lounged against the wall, his demonic invisibility in place as he waited. Kasria arrived at a full out sprint, her eyes wild and concern etched in every facet of her body. He watched her scan the obviously empty space concern fading to confusion. He appeared right by the door almost as if he had walked through it. "Kasria! Thank the Gods!"

She latched on to him with a look of relief on her face. "Zadon. What happened?!"

He strode to her one arm going around her shoulders in a comforting gesture. "He was distracted when some of the older air shifter males started a fight over resources. We tried to diffuse it but the fight grew too large. I warned him we should have brought in back up."

He sighed heavily as he reached into his pocket with his free hand pulling out a rag drenched with a sleeping draft. Kasria didn't have time to register the movement before the rag descended over her mouth and nose. His superior demonic strength ensured that she couldn't break out of his grip.

It was a good struggle. She did her best trying to get out, her fingers elongating into claws, but the potion did its job before her full transition. He hoisted her now limp form over his shoulder traveling down the empty servants' corridor to the safety of the dank dungeon. He went to the deepest prison appropriately outfitted with chains and all the tools for his fun.

He chained her ankles to the ground and waited for her to wake. He had no worry about her using her powers or shifting due to the crystals that ringed the room.

These crystals were especially rare, only growing in the wall that separated the realms. In Dodsfell they existed everywhere. Yet due to their power dampening effect on mortals he wasn't surprised they were scarce on this side of the barrier. He sat on the ground back against the door. He had ensured that if Lucian came looking Valri would distract him.

It took roughly twenty minutes before she started stirring. He began to toy with a dagger flipping it casually in front of him as he waited for her to realize what was transpiring.

She sat up slowly rubbing her eyes and blinking confused. "Zadon what is happening? Where are we?"

He sneered at her. "Ah her Majesty has awoken. Welcome back. We are currently in your new quarters."

She looked around her fear taking root in her eyes sending a thrill down his spine. "Zadon. Where is Lucian? Is he okay? I can't reach his wolf."

"He is fine, I expect. He went to the camp with Ulfur. He shall be back presently. You see, I was supposed to accompany him." He stood walking around the dank room excitement building as she turned to keep him in her eyesight.

"Yet I knew it was much more important to take care of a pest problem."

"He's fine?"

"Yes, Kasria."

His mood drifted down as her fear seemed to ease.

"You think there is a pest problem?" He watched as she did her best to school her face and take control.

He began laughing. "Yes, Kasria there is indeed a pest problem, and it begins and ends with you."

He crouched in front of her, still out of reach of her claws. Her face stayed remarkably impassive, yet her feet pulled ever so slightly as if testing the chains.

He grinned, clapping as he stood. "Now that you understand why we are here, let's begin."

The chain rustled a bit as she followed his movement. He had stashed a small cart of essentials in the corner and took the opportunity to survey the contents. A small vial with an oil rumored to be poisonous to wolves, a whip, a carving knife and the ability to create a fire. He debated a fire, it would be fun but could draw unwanted attention. He grabbed the vial and turned back to the slut in chains. "I heard a rumor about wolf shifters once in Dodsfell. They have a weakness which Goddess Duella created to anger the God Culgan."

Her eyes widened true fear showing through.

"Ahh so it is true to some extent. Well, let's see to what level, shall we?"

She scurried back as far as she could manage with the chain. "You know he will come looking for me. If he finds you with me in that state he will know."

Zadon's face hurt with his glee. "My dear. I have been alive long enough that I know how to clean up my own mess. The Gods know I have been taking care of the Prince's messes since I met him."

He grabbed her foot, trapped by the chain and swiped a line of the oil up her calf. Her skirt riding up with her crawling.

"If you hurt me, you hurt him! He's your best friend. Your brother!"

Zadon watched her calf intently. It had begun to redden, small bubbles popping through. Kasria shifted once more to sit on her hands.

"The urge to scratch must be immense. How does it feel? Is it hot?"

"Fuck. Off."

Zadon clucked his tongue in mock disappointment. "That's no way to speak to the one in charge of how much pain you're in."

He went invisible causing her to gasp. He rushed her slashing with his knife leaving a cut across her dress. He pouted when she refused to scream. Moving quickly he grabbed her hand and forced her down. She fought a gurgling strangled cry as he leveraged his weight onto her arm. He plunged his dagger through her palm into the grout lines between the stones anchoring her at three points face up. Pulling another dagger from his boot he rematerialized as he pried her remaining hand out from her middle. She gasped tears streaming down her face. "Punishments aren't meant to be enjoyable."

She sobbed so hard, she hiccupped her body shuddering.

He brought out a third knife tracing her body with the point, goosebumps following in the wake. "Now to business. You are a pest having created more work for me to fix than you realize. You see before he met you." He sliced her shallowly across her abdomen smiling at the blood. "I had begun an experiment."

She groaned loudly as he pressed deeply, loving the gush that emerged with the blade. "Do you know what happens to the average mortal who ingests demons' blood?"

He paused waiting for an answer. "You know answering questions is good manners. Do you need another punishment so soon?"

She gasped, shaking her head. "No I don't know, you bastard."

He nodded, accepting her answer. "Normal mortals experience immense mind-bending pain. Hmm... perhaps we should see if you can tell me if a knife or ingesting the blood is worse. A thought for later perhaps. Regardless, Lucian drank my blood without experiencing the pain."

He watched her process this. She gasped as he sliced again. Nicking her skin while completely opening the dress leaving her body available to his knife.

"You're the darkness." It came out as a whisper, but it had his blood freezing.

"Darkness?"

She began shaking her head, lips clamped tightly shut.

"No. No you must tell me, or I shall see how many cuts it takes to make you talk." He wanted her to talk, otherwise he would just feed her the blood and allow her to shake and scream in pain. He needed to know the depths that his blood had changed Lucian.

Kasria slammed her eyes shut unwilling to listen to his demands.

"Cut it is. Let's count them out.

One

Two

Three."

By ten her skin was glistening with a sheen of sweat. Tears streaming, her eyes crying as her lip trembled.

"Eleven. Twelve..." By twenty she was bleeding without gushing and as he looked deeper the cuts were actually healing. He scanned the room reassuring himself that the crystals remained. They did which left only one option.

"He fucking mated you! You've had the bond recognized." It would account for her healing without her power. The bond relying on Lucian's power to heal. Zadon's mind raced, his timeline with Kasria had just shortened. Lucian would be able to sense her much stronger with a recognized soulbond connection than just the unrecognized bond.

She coughed her body spasming with the effort. "Yes, we did."

"Bitch. I give you one last opportunity to choose. You can tell me about this darkness, and I'll make your death quick and painless. Otherwise I will draw it out long and painful causing you both to suffer."

Tears fell from her eyes as she realized there would be no escape from death. "The darkness is a being that lives in his mind. It's tangible and it fights his wolf, preying on him."

Glee filled him, coursing through his blood like fire. "So I am a part of him."

"Yes." She sounded angry and despondent. He sat back on his heels thinking it through. He couldn't be separated from Lucian. How interesting.

He pushed her sweaty hair away from her face. "I always keep my promises."

He leaned over her bringing the knife up to her throat.

"Tell him I love him. I'll see him at the end."

Zadon winked at her as the knife slid home into her throat, her lifeblood draining so quickly the bond couldn't heal her.

thirty-eight

LUCIAN

PALION - DRAK - YEAR 7558

The pain searing through his body was unbearable. He had no cognitive understanding on how he even reached the palace. All he did know for certain was he had to find Kasria. His wolf was frantically pacing in his mind. The pack howled echoing in the recesses, crying out for her.

He rushed to their room convinced some mistake had happened. She would appear from the bathing chamber rosy pink, with brunette hair clumped and dripping, a laugh at all the fuss.

He flung open the door, her scent rushing out the air cold and empty. His body froze, unable to cross the threshold. Ulfur slammed into his back, but Lucian gripped the frame groaning as he took on Ulfur's weight. Baryn skidded into sight at the end of the hall, his face eerily pale.

"Where?" His voice wasn't even his own as the monsters in his mind surged around him trying to snuff him out for good.

"Lucian. Brother. No." Baryn's face crumpled, tears pouring. "You can't," A sob ripped through him. "See her. Not like this."

Lucian rushed him and before Ulfur could stop him, he gripped Baryn around the throat squeezing. Baryn gasped, choking on tears, saliva and the need for air. Mentally he cried to the pack echoing for all to hear. "Gardens."

Lucian dropped him, not even stopping to see if he was okay before sprinting all out to the gardens. A crowd had gathered all facing away from what awaited him. He couldn't stop to study the morbid picture of the palace inhabitants all studiously keeping their back turned from the death that waited further in. It was a show of respect while staying away from the impurity that came with death.

The world ground to a halt as he neared, the smell of blood overwhelming that of the newly opening flowers. Her body had been laid atop a bed of winter roses still in bloom, her dress garishly sliced open exposing her to the elements. Half healed cuts, still draining, staining the roses.

He could almost convince himself it was an elaborate trick if not for the jagged cut across her throat gaping open. Her eyes, glassy and unseeing. He had no memory of moving yet he suddenly caressed her blood-soaked hand tears falling unbidden down upon her face. Her body was rigid, cold and bluing on the edges of all the cuts that littered her body.

"Blankets! Now!" He yelled it out and somebody scrambled away.

Zadon's dark voice broke into his mind. "We should contact the temple milord. There is a timing to this."

"Get her some fucking blankets."

Someone shoved soft blankets into his hand, and he breathed deep. At least until his hands couldn't stop shaking to spread them.

"Highness. Perhaps you would allow me." Suzu hiccupped as she held out her hands, tears streaming down her face.

He nodded the movement foreign and jerky, handing it to her. He watched like a hawk as she unfolded it carefully covering Kasria's indecent exposure.

Once she was covered, he felt his lungs open up more fully.

Zadon pressed in from behind. "Sire."

"Suzu. Get the temple Oba not an acolyte. Ulfur." A grunt followed. "Clear these people back. I want a fucking report from every damn guard on duty."

He stared unseeing at his love's face trying desperately to turn back time and find a way for her to breathe once more.

thirty-nine

SUZU

PALION - DRAK - YEAR 7558

Her heart broke for Lucian and her mind became frantic to keep Belvina and Ulfur safe. She had a strong desire to keep them both near her at all times, but with Ulfur's position in the court that was impossible. Instead she gripped Belvina's arm silently asking her to come with her to the temple. The journey to the temple was swift, the air dense as if the Gods mourned their loss as well.

Tixdarr acolytes dressed in hooded maroon robes were frantic running about much like an upturned ant hill. Suzu would almost find great joy in it if not for the devastating reason for her visit. Unsurprisingly due to the amount of people who saw Kasria in her final state, the rumors had beaten them to the temple. Suzu squared her shoulders and approached the one stationary hooded figure near the door, "We need to see Oba Kana."

"Of course Miss." The acolyte nodded once before disappearing through a hallway.

They didn't have long to wait before another faceless acolyte was leading them through the temple. Suzu tightened her hand on Belvina's, barely concealing her eye roll at the audacity when Kana came into view. The Oba of Tixdarr lounged indolently on a throne decorated in demons and flame motifs. She was dressed in burgundy robes that covered her from head to toe. Her face obscured by veils intricately anchored in her hair to allude to demon horns.

"What do I owe the pleasure of this interruption?"

"The Court of Palion needs your services. Your distinct services." Suzu heavily emphasized. It wouldn't do for Kasria's service to be overseen by an acolyte.

"Did the King die? How unfortunate." It almost sounded like Kana was amused.

Suzu's mind blanked with rage. This woman knew. If her acolytes knew so did she. Suzu took a menacing step forward but was halted by a voice behind her.

"The Luna of the Wolves was murdered." Belvina's voice had developed a steel edge Suzu had never heard from her before.

Kana tutted. "While that is unfortunate for her, an upper acolyte can manage her service and preparation just fine."

Kana raised her hand to dismiss them, but Suzu breathed deeply, affecting a tone that sounded sickly sweet even to her own ears. "It would be such a shame if you found yourself in need on this mortal plane. This temple is beholden to the Kingdom of Palion. After this level of insult you'll be lucky if Prince Lucian ever looks your way again."

Kana waved her hands dismissively "What do I care about a trumped-up Prince in the larger scheme of things. After all I have the patronage of a God."

Suzu swallowed her retort, pride swelling as Belvina took

two steps forward, acid dripping from her words. "Perhaps you don't know the old ways of the wolf. Lord Culgan had a distinct way of dealing with our dead. Ceremonies and rituals that have been passed down by the Alphas. His Highness is too beside himself to remember but The Elder has been sent for. We. Don't. Need. You." She shook out her skirts dramatically. "Once the people see your merely an option perhaps your God may deign to replace you."

Suzu delivered the smallest of curtsies toward Kana before leading Belvina toward the door. Before the door could open Kana clapped twice. "Very well. I shall attend this no names ceremony."

Suzu whipped her head around, eyes narrowing. "You will show your respect for the one that would have been Queen. Her name was Kasria Lykos."

Kana strode toward them. "You see little one. I have the ear of a God. Kasria was never to be Queen. Another is coming fit for that role."

Belvina growled and Suzu struggled to cap her emotions. "And you are proof that even the Gods make mistakes."

Kana's laughter followed them down to the main doors where four acolytes waited, a carrying board between them. They wore the deep red cloaks hoods pulled to obscure their faces.

* * *

It had taken a few hours to extricate Lucian from Kasria's body long enough that the acolytes could wrap her and place her on the carrying board. Belvina and a few other female wolves gathered fresh roses from the other gardens to nestle around her. Suzu ran to get a Palion flag and stole a small tiara. Harold would never notice it gone and Lucian would love to see the respect if he was even capable of true sight.

Zadon hadn't left Lucian's side since she was found and Suzu knew it would lead to issues, but she didn't have the strength to care. The demon had an unknown agenda that somehow Kasria was opposing, at one point she would have to take up the mantle. The procession through the city tore at her emotional reserves. She held both Belvina's and Ulfur's hands, pulling the strength she could.

In the temple Kana waited at the altar, the spot of honor for Kasria's body decked out befitting a Queen. Suzu breathed a little easier knowing she wouldn't have to spill blood in a temple. Kana even referenced Kasria as the beloved Queen to be, the people's choice. Cursing whoever stole such a gem from the mortal plane.

"It is believed the soul stays near the body for two days searching their mind for the answer to one question. Should they be released to the Gods for reincarnation or stay within the parameters of Dodsfell to await the loved ones that still walk Baelia?" Kana paused head down, giving gravity to Kasria's choice.

Lucian walked up to the body despite the protests of the acolytes nearest him. "Kas whatever you choose find peace. It's what you gave me."

He collapsed next to the dias head bowed as sobs wracked his body. Ulfur squeezed Suzu's hand and smiled weakly at Belvina on her other side before walking up to join Lucian standing at his back in guard stance facing the crowd. Blocking their view of the future king losing his composure. Baryn was a step behind Ulfur settling next to him. Juro, Ulfur's second, joined them. The men using their bodies to shield their leader in his weakness.

Suzu couldn't stop her own sobs.

forty

LUCIAN

PALION - DRAK - YEAR 7558

> Wolves have always had ways of dealing with the world that predates even the Gods. Once Gods came onto the scene the Wolves were very skeptical as to the effectiveness that they would hold on their community. Culgan had his work cut out for him. He managed to win them over by honoring their original traditions. Through Culgan the strictly traditional wolves could still find acceptance into Dodsfell and the Void beyond if needed. It gave the wolves a way to live authentically.
>
> ~Culgan Temple Archives

The world was a haze. Nothing seemed real anymore. The golden light that protected him from the monsters had been extinguished and he couldn't for the life of him understand why.

The people around him sounded like buzzing all monotonous and boring, the words unable to sink into his head. He couldn't even be bothered to care that they never left him alone. Someone was always there talking, buzzing around. Suddenly a dim glow appeared in his mind. Illuminating the dark creatures that dwelled within, sinking their talons into his brain.

He picked his head up trying to figure out where the glow came from. His room was full of people. The days of solitude were over. He suspected Belvina had orchestrated it so he would never be truly alone, at least not for a while.

Suzu, Ulfur and Belvina were all huddled together just leaning against one another. Zadon stood on the edge of the room, his eyes glued to Lucian's every move. Juro stood to the side huddled with other members of the guard whispering furiously. Only one other person sat despondent in the room. Baryn. Kasria's brother. He took a minute to study the man and began to see the similarities between them that had gone unnoticed.

Baryn had the same color hair, shorn back but the color couldn't be masked. He also had the same shaped ears. A small and insignificant detail but one that stood out to him. Lucian fell onto the seat next to him, their shoulders bumping together.

"Baryn." His voice was foreign even to his own ears.

Baryn brought red rimmed eyes up to meet his. "Yes Milord."

"I need you. You need to stay with us, be a part of the inner court." He paused, swallowing back a sob. "Keep me on Kasria's path. She had a vision. You... you can help me."

Baryn's mouth fell open, his eyes wide.

"Please?"

"Yes! Wherever you go I will follow and guide you towards her light."

Lucian nodded his eyes closing as the golden light shone a bit more. It wasn't strong but it was in the corner of his consciousness enough that perhaps he could fight the darkness.

forty-one

HAROLD

PALION - DRAK - YEAR 7558

The over perfumed cloying air clogged his lungs. His mind fought for logic as he witnessed his son take the spot of honor next to the dead, not him. Whoever had created this ceremony had to have studied his late Queens passing to the realm beyond.

The colors were all formal Palion, the flag draped across her linen shrouded body. Shock rippled through him at the glint of metal near where her head was. A crown had been placed there. A shudder pulsated through his mind, shaking the foundations of his resolve. He needed it to stay present to live in the now.

Another wave of sickly sweet rose scent assaulted his nose, and his mind reeled, unable to discern the past from the present. His knuckles went on the sides of his chair going white with the effort to know where he was, when he was. He clamped his eyes shut, breathing deep desperately trying to recalibrate to his surroundings.

All he could hear was a buzz. The words his son spoke lost

to it. A touch on his arm had him jolting a small scream escaping.

"Milord? Milord, are you okay?"

Harold blinked rapidly. "What? Yes?"

The man sitting next to him nodded, giving him a small sad smile. Harold inclined his head slightly. Before his mind slipped back to memories of *her*. His Queen. The blonde curls, always scented with honey and oranges. His mouth could practically taste them. The roses she cut and spread throughout the palace all the time. The memories were so strong he had missed the temple emptying.

A dark voice sounded from above him.

"Sire? Are you feeling alright? Shall I call a medic?"

Harold had enough power of thought to look up only for his eyes to land on Zadon's face. He tried to wave Zadon off but didn't have the strength to speak, the emotional tidal wave drowning him.

"Oh no, let's take you back to the palace. I shall find someone to aid you."

Zadon lifted him by his arms and guided him somewhat forcefully to the carriage. Harold was grateful that he had no need to think, instead he could live in the depths of his memory.

He wasn't sure how much time truly had passed when his hand was wrapped around a glass. Zadon's dark voice interrupting the numb void in his mind.

"Drink up sire. This will help."

He looked at the glass, it appeared like amber liquid. Harold shrugged, not caring, taking a long swallow. It took mere seconds before the world disappeared to dreamland.

He blinked and another glass was shoved in his hand, the burn in his throat the only lasting memory.

———

PALION - ANIT - YEAR 7558

"Sire?" The soft familiar voice of Suzu broke through the warm blankets of black.

He sought out the voice, eyes blinking rapidly. "Suzu?" His voice cracking from disuse.

"It is you! We need to get you out of here."

"Where am I?" Confusion filtered into the darkness swamping him.

"The Southern Tower. I've been searching for you for months, ever since Kasria's rite." He could make out her shadowed form hunting around the room. "What did he do to you?"

Harold heard the twinkling of glass before she gasped. "He's drugging you! This could knock a beast flat out. Come on Sire, the kingdom is relying on you."

She was back at his side tugging on his arm desperately.

"No. Suzu. Stop. Listen child." Her tugging slowed as she looked at him. His vision returned enough to see the outline of her face. "Leave me here. I can't. I can't live without her anymore and this darkness is rather comforting while I wait." He patted her hand tenderly and closed his eyes.

forty-two

SUZU

PALION - ANIT - YEAR 7558

Suzu hesitated. She should talk to Ulfur and Belvina. They both frequently told her no to making big decisions alone, but time wasn't on her side. She palmed her dagger and leaned in whispering. "Do you want to join her? Join your Queen?"

Harold's blood-streaked gaze locked on her a hunger flickering in the depths. It was the first time since she found him that the gaze looked clear and sane.

"Yes."

"I'm so sorry to be the one to do this." Her hand quivered fear shooting through her at the idea of rocketing herself and her loved ones into a magical unknown. *What would happen with no Rite?* Yet she couldn't leave him at the mercy of Zadon.

"Suzu. It is best this way. It has to be you. You can fight him. You must fight him."

She took a deep breath and nodded, bringing the knife up and plunging it straight into the pulsing vein at his neck.

Hot copper liquid spewed all over her and she cursed her

lack of foresight. Harold shook but she maintained her position holding the knife there keeping the hole in his neck open despite the Great Power trying to save him. Harold for his credit tried to stay still. His jerking minimal. Life drained away from his eyes and his body slumped away from her. Her heart remained heavy and burdened.

A few moments after the life finished flickering in Harold's eyes a sharp pain seared through Suzu's temple causing her to drop the knife. Her bloody hands reached up grabbing her head as the pain blinded her to everything.

Her eyes slammed shut and she felt her consciousness get ripped from her mortal body. Forcibly pulled towards a lake of green power far below. She pulled back trying to move her mental consciousness to get it to go where she wanted and avoid a collision with the power below her. Nothing she did could stop it.

As she entered the lake of the Great Power of the Land it soaked through her mental consciousness. Pain ricocheted around her mind, telling her that Ulfur and Belvina were battling this power themselves. The green power covered her, and she felt a suffocating feeling as if she was drowning even though her mortal body was collapsed next to Harold's corpse. The green transitioned to yellow and then to orange before she could finally stop the forward momentum.

She stalled unsure what to do without the guiding presence of an Oba. As the time continued, she felt an overpowering sense of urgency swell within her. If enough time passed her mortal body would be found with the corpse of the king and she would be finished.

Suddenly her mind filled with a vision of Belvina curled on the ground of their chamber whimpering, sobs wracking her. "Suzu. Suzu. Suzu." Her hands clutching at her heart.

Ulfur's chiseled face filled her vision clutching his head as he took staggered pained steps in a familiar hall muttering, "Suzu where the fuck are you?"

She pushed against the magic a new determination swelled in her. Surprise filled her as it moved out of her way much like water moved when swimming. She headed back toward the green hoping once there a path would appear to lead her back to her body.

The slog through the lake of power left her mentally exhausted and ready to admit defeat. Regret crested through her, perhaps Ulfur and Belvina would still survive her loss, since they had each other to cling to. There was just no way for her to get back to her body.

It was at that point she started to feel phantom sensations where her body should have been. Tingles, electricity and heat all flowed through her shoulders and across her face. She gasped as Ulfur's gruff voice filled her mental awareness.

"Kitten, what trouble have you gotten into this time?" She could feel him kissing along where her cheek and ear should have been. "Come back to us you stubborn spy. Show me just one more time how superior cats are. What's the saying?" He paused. She noticed that his voice sounded a bit louder enabling her to hear the cracking anguish.

"Cats have nine lives. Prove it now Kitten. Fuck. Please just breathe."

She coughed. Her mind slamming into her body, surprised it felt so small to her now. Ulfur was curled around her, uncaring of the blood and the remains lying next to them.

"Come on Kit. We gotta get back to Beauty before they come looking for him."

Suzu nodded, not trusting her voice, emotions clogging her throat. Exhaustion pulled at her bones causing her body to be unsteady. Ulfur placed himself right next to her, being the post she needed to lean on. "We have to get rid of the shoes and socks.

So they can't trace us back to our home." He nodded merely leaning down and removing the offending items, helping her to stay steady on a clean patch floor free from Harold's life blood.

Once Ulfur's shoes were removed he swept her into his arms. Heading to the main door, the one where he had stumbled through apparently, as it was standing open. "No, no. Take the servants' passage."

"Where?"

"Over there." She pointed toward a large picture hanging near the fireplace. She balanced their shoes in her arms while Ulfur carried her through the secret passage swiftly making sure they got home safe.

forty-three

SUZU

PALION - ANIT - YEAR 7558

Ulfur placed her on the ground outside of their apartment and together they limped inside. She was eager to lay eyes on Belvina, what she didn't expect was a slap. She barely had time to process the beautiful face in front of her when Belvina's hand flew. The pain, sharp and sudden with enough force her head twisted.

"Okay. Was that necessary Beauty?" Ulfur's gruff voice cut through the sting.

"You felt it Ulfur. I know you did. I could feel it through you. She was dying! She could have thought of us and made a different decision to begin with, so she wasn't on deaths door!"

Suzu could see the hurt and confusion marring Belvina's face. She sighed deeply, rubbing absently at her cheek. "It was unavoidable. I did consider you, I just had no time."

Suzu watched as Belvina took in the bloodied clothes and limping nature of both of them. Her face closing off as she waited. Ulfur's hand landed on Suzu's shoulder giving it a squeeze.

"Belvina if you felt it through me then you know it was unavoidable. What we need to know now is what happens next. She's landed us in rather hot water."

The weight of their reality lay heavily on her shoulders. She dropped her cloak on the crackling fire watching it burn before she looked back at her spouses. "I found Harold. Four months of tireless searching and he was imprisoned in the Southern tower. Zadon kept him drugged with sleeping draughts and medicinal potions." She turned back to the fire and tossed in her socks the snapping crackles making her flinch just a bit.

"He had no fight left. Something at Kasria's ceremony triggered a mental break of which he refused to come out of. At least not without his Queen."

She turned tear filled eyes to her partners. "True to demonic rumors, Zadon didn't care about his emotional spiral. I don't have any hard evidence but my gut tells me the demon would have tortured that sad man."

Belvina had tears in her own eyes. "But you've only told stories about how mean he is. Why help him? Why care? Why risk us?"

Suzu took a shuddering breath, her hands itched to hide her face but the dried blood caking them had her hesitating. Instead she began to unlace the corset. "I won't be like him. He was cruel and vicious, while at the same time you could see moments of caring. A trap I foresaw myself falling into if I just walked away."

Ulfur spoke up, "We wouldn't have seen you like that Suzu. Never. We know you."

"I would have though. At the end of the day I have to be able to sleep with the decisions I have made. This idea wasn't the best, but I couldn't stand for him to be a pawn for the demon."

Belvina nodded once, her face an unreadable mask. "Don't you dare burn your clothes. Shed them in the corner and then come take a bath."

Ulfur paced "We aren't done yet though. She killed the bloody King. She unlocked the Great Power of the Land without the guidance of the Oba. What the hell happens next? What are we?" He gestured dramatically to all of them.

Suzu stripped out of her plain black clothes and trudged to the bathing chamber, her shoulders slumped. She had no answers right now. She didn't understand how they had survived or what they would do next. She paused at the threshold slightly surprised at the kindness Belvina showed her. The tub was filled with hot soapy water, the air vibrating with the heat. Belvina walked past her, back into the living chambers placing a chaste kiss on her forehead as she went. "Take your time love."

Suzu watched her leave, smiling that she left the door ajar just in case Suzu needed one of them. It also held the benefit of aiding her in overhearing their conversation.

"Give her a minute to herself. We all know the obvious danger ahead but she's telling the truth and trying her best. You will respect her space, or I will have you answer for it."

Suzu muffled a giggle as she made out Ulfur's grumbling. Belvina the protector warmed her heart just as Ulfur her savior did. Yet should she be the ruler? Or should she hold the power for Aurelia, if she ever even came back? She sat in the scented water mulling it over, until the air calmed, and the bubbles disappeared, the water cool even to her wet skin. She scrubbed the blood out from under her nails and rinsed her hair and face. Then she rose resolve in her desire for the next step.

She wrapped the warm bath robe around her as she entered their living space. Belvina sat huddled, a piece of bloodied clothing gripped in her hands. As she watched Belvina used a seed of power to obliterate the blood present on the material.

"I didn't know you could do that." Her words must have broken the trance Belvina found herself in.

Belvina's chocolate eyes shot to hers and a smile filled her face. "There you are."

Suzu smiled. "I appreciate the time to come back to myself. Now it's time we plan. As a family."

She didn't need to search far to see Ulfur's warm gaze, as he nodded. "Family."

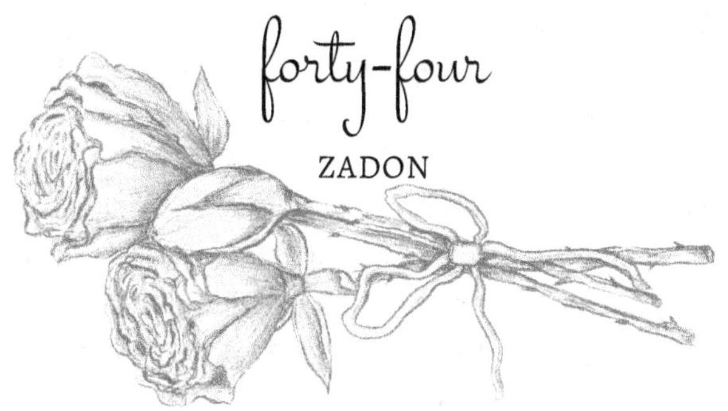

forty-four

ZADON

PALION - DRAK - YEAR 7568

"When you die your soul is presented with two options. The first is obvious, believe in the Gods and go forth allowing Tiva and Oxius find you a new vessel for you to live again in a new body to continue your souls mission. The second option is one that is difficult and only the most determined of souls opt for it. You can choose to wander Dodsfell waiting for your soulbond, or child to join you. Whatever it is that ties you to the mortal world you can watch through the veil of Dodsfell. However the one thing that these souls don't realize is they don't actually get to reunite with their loved ones as is touted by the Tixdarr temple. Instead once the object of their obsession passes on as well the soul that chose Dodsfell simply ceases to exist. There is a hypothesis that those souls get recycled into demons. One may never know the truth.

~Tixdarr Temple Archives Kana's personal Journal.

Zadon stomped the well-worn path next to the wall separating the realms. It had been somewhere around nine years and he couldn't understand why they bothered waiting for the Berrid Princess. Dodsfell wouldn't release her. If it was inclined to do so she would already be back in the land of the living.

Yet this was one of the many things that Lucian had doggedly refused to give up after Kasria's demise. Zadon reached the end of the wall and turned again walking back the way he had come mulling over the time he had endured.

He had pulled Lucian back to the darkside easily enough. Many victims had fallen to him in the time since Kasria's death and each instance had left Zadon giddy at the prospect. It was only a matter of time before Tixdarr noticed this abnormal mortal and demanded Lucian's presence in Dodsfell which would usher Zadon back home.

There was also the looming mystery surrounding Harold's death. While Lucian didn't seem to care, his attitude when not driven by the rage and bloodthirsty monster, rather lackluster and despondent. Zadon understood just how vitally important it was to figure out. Over the years there were signs someone close to them held the power. Things growing where it was impossible, roots appearing in crowded rooms, the entire ground shaking the very palace itself. Yet for reasons he could not understand, whoever it was that held the power never stepped forward to claim the throne as would have been proper. A chime sounded, somewhere far above Zadon. As if the clouds were ringing bells. Zadon froze.

Up ahead was the hole in Palion's wall separating the realms. He blinked. Not trusting his own eyes as a boot followed by a skinny calf pushed its way through. The magic rippling as it released the individual into Baelia.

He stayed frozen to the spot as the rest of the woman was released. Her blue-black hair, a beacon to her heritage. It looked to be the length of her waist but was matted and dirty. Her clothes were patched and ragged, a sword strapped to her back and a long dagger to her thigh.

"Aurelia." He whispered it still in disbelief at his good fortune. Perhaps Tixdarr was watching.

She whirled the sudden movement throwing her off balance causing a noticeable wobble. "What?" Her face dropped, the paleness getting paler as she focused on him. "How the fuck did I find a demon in Baelia?"

Zadon couldn't help the laughter that bubbled out. "Luck I suppose." He shrugged. "The good news is I am a demon who is also a part of the Palion court."

She crossed her arms and studied him, not flinching when the clatter of a staff sounded behind her. "I don't want anything to do with the Palion court."

"Ah. Well I don't believe you get a choice."

He watched as she flexed her fingers, obviously itching for a fight. If he remembered correctly, she was a hot-tempered individual. "You don't understand demon. I have spent ten years being dictated to. I will be doing whatever I want from here on out. That includes leaving this kingdom."

Zadon chuckled as he took a few steps forward. "I wonder what all you were told to do." His voice dropped a few octaves, the dark he kept in firm check leaking out. "What wicked things did my kind manage to do to a flower such as you?"

Aurelia's gaze hardened. "Come closer, perhaps I'll show you."

Faster than any mortal he had seen she had her sword unsheathed pointing down.

"Are you going to skewer the royal advisor? The Prince

won't take that kindly." He took another step before releasing a long whistle. Aurelia stiffened but didn't budge. Guards flooded the area, closing the circle around the Princess trapping her. Her eyes flicked a bit tracking those guards in her direct line of sight.

"I suppose you can have a few options." Zadon leaned against the magic encased wall, the buzzing of power a comforting tingle. "The first option is," he held up a finger. "you can go back through the wall to my brethren. The second option is you fight all of these guards alone and then fight me. Or finally you can just come willingly to the palace."

Aurelia hummed in her throat. "What does he want from me?"

"Your ever-loving gratitude and lifelong loyalty as his Queen."

A shudder racked through her. "That will never willingly happen."

"I'll settle for unwillingly." Zadon shrugged. "I'm not that picky."

She turned quickly, engaging the guard directly behind her. The surprise attack gave her the advantage, and she quickly dispatched him. *Weak mortals.* Zadon chuckled as she continued to fight.

She held her own impressively well as the guards closed in. He tapped his foot as she growled and panted. In the end she took five of the guards out before they managed to disarm her.

She screamed in frustration as a guard forced her to her knees tieing her hands behind her.

"Now, now Princess. All it will take is some time amongst the civilized and that feral quality will deaden."

She snarled at him, her lip curling as she spat at the ground. "Wanna make a wager on that?"

Zadon's face grew into a huge smile. He motioned two of

the remaining guards forward following the hissing spitting viper of a woman towards the palace dungeons. *Life just got more interesting.*

a note to the reader

arling Mortal Friends,
As all weak hearted mortals you are undoubtedly screaming at the injustice of cliffhangers. Unfortunately for you this is the end for now. Patience will be required for what's coming next. After all, as you mortals are always saying. The good only comes to those who wait. Or some such nonsense. Be prepared for the final installment of the Dodsfell Books within the Baelian Empire in Early 2026.

~Tixdarr Lord of the Dead

To The Mortals Who Dream of More,

The death of Kasria made it impossible for me to leverage my Godly attributes to their full effect. I am hoping this finds the right hands. The Gods are stuck in the Void and we need assistance. Lucian may be beyond me but perhaps I can funnel gifts to Aurelia or those closest to her.

~Lord Culgan God of the Wolves

CHAPTER ONE - AURELIA - YEAR 7568

The dank cold of the cell was trying to settle into her bones. She could feel it laying on her skin like a slimy blanket. She did her best to ignore that sensation in favor of the many other new yet oddly old sensations vying for her attention in her mind.

The darkness that had become second nature to her still took up a large portion of her magical well. Though now she could feel other styles of magic thrumming beneath her skin begging to be used. She breathed deep, sorting through the feelings until heat flooded her keeping the slimy dankness of the dungeon permanently at bay.

A deep sigh of satisfaction emerged as her eyes fluttered open. Now that a semblance of comfort had been achieved it was time to assess her newest predicament. Somehow a demon appeared to be in the upper reaches of Palion's court. Something Kygoss and his birdies hadn't uncovered during her training time. Perhaps this demon was a red one similar to Balthor and thus cunning would be how he achieved his position in the court.

She stared around the cell noting a small window in the wall she leaned against. It was positioned too far up for her small height of five feet four inches. There was a rudimentary bench which she rested on. It didn't take long for her to come up with a plan. She studied the hallway outside her barred wall, waiting to see if there was anything happening. A few minutes passed and nothing happened so she pushed the bench until it rested directly under the window.

She didn't expect much because the window was small and located at the ground level. She could make out boots, wheels, horse hooves and in the far distance mountains. She hopped back down to the ground. It was possible to scream and probably elicit some sort of reaction yet there was no guarantee it would bring helpful attention. Ultimately she needed a way to escape this damn kingdom. Her goal was to head to Meltem Islands and hide out, perhaps grow a garden and generally avoid all living creatures. If she did that then the days of pain and torture would finally be done.

Visions of the scaly demons floated through her mind causing her blood to spike, fear coating her mouth. Her hair rustled, rising. It had her mind stumbling over the carousel of memories. Her hair continued to float, which due to the mats and dirt felt awkward. *How is it moving?* She whirled around yet no one was there. Her shirt began to tug around her body and she closed her eyes, panic rising. Perhaps it had finally happened; she had lost her mind.

Finally broken.

A thrum took up in her blood. Her eyes snapped open as the wind picked up leaves that were moldering in the corner. The wind all but attacked her. Swirling around her invading her every pore.

Aurelia giggled. New memories assaulting her mind. Ones that she had locked deep in her soul. Filled with her experimenting with her inherent gift with the wind. It had been her first ever magical exploration and if this reaction was anything to go by it had missed her.

Aurelia took some deep breaths centering herself before rolling through some of the basic air magic exercises she could remember, her fingers itching to experiment further. A clanging on the bars of her cage had her tucking her hands behind her, a ready glare directed at the newcomer.

A blonde man stood his hands tucked into his pants pockets observing her. The demon who had brought her was stationed just behind. It clicked then who this blonde was. He didn't resemble the drawing Kygoss had once shown her. Instead his face was hollow, eyes haunted, perhaps more than even hers were.

"The Palion Pup in the flesh. What an honor." The words came out dry, "Looking a little worse for wear Lucian."

The blonde didn't even twitch as if he couldn't hear her. The demon however growled. "His name is Lucian Ronnet and he is the King."

"Oh good! Then you no longer need me." She shrugged, examining her fingernails carefully. "After all this arrangement was only created to ensure the Pup there inherited." She caught the demon tightening his fists and smirked.

Lucian shifted angling to glance between them. "Zadon,

wanna explain why the Princess of Drakore is in the dungeon instead of a room befitting her station."

She watched the interplay curiously as Zadon flushed. "She was practically feral when I found her. Her powers are an unknown factor and I didn't trust your safety."

Lucian cocked an eyebrow and turned back to her. She tilted her head mocking his curiosity. "What is your power?"

"Vast." She grinned.

"I'm sure seeing as you survived ten years in Dodsfell when many more deserving souls have perished in the mortal realm." He glanced at the demon who she surmised was named Zadon. "She can't look like that."

Zadon merely nodded his agreement. "We can have the ladies attend her."

"We could, but can they handle her?"

"Can you?" She asked it with sugary sweetness falsely dripping from the words.

Lucian ignored her. "We need to find the appropriate motivation and then perhaps she could be convinced to abide by the plan."

"Motivation. That is a great idea." She lifted her hands digging into the well of air power that had begun to grow within her since she arrived in the mortal realm. She lobbed the air at Zadon's chest flinging him into the wall opposite her cage. "You see there's one thing you haven't figured out. I have nothing you can use against me. As far as I know, I don't even have anything you want. So be a dear and use your mangy paw and let me go before I play with more powers."

Zadon's eyes were bugging out of his sockets but she turned her glare on Lucian waiting, hoping he made a decision before her fledgling grasp on her power broke.

Lucian grunted. "Point made. Put him down."

She merely loosened the hold so he could breath, not

releasing him to the ground, merely raising her eyebrow. "It's time for some truth, Lucian. Or open the damn door."

Lucian crossed his arms and grunted. "Fine. You are still needed. I am merely King in name not title. We are waiting until I can get a suitable bride tied to the Great Power of the Land to strengthen Palion. Hence where you come in."

She nodded her mind stuck on how in ten years he had the same problem he did before. "Palion is slow in problem solving." She shrugged. "Get a different princess. There's no true reason for me to help you."

"There is." Zadon squawked.

She shoved her power harder against the demon. "Hush now the adults are talking, not the pets."

"We have him." Zadon's continued squawking had her pushing the wind harder against him.

Aurelia's brow furrowed. "Him? Him who? Really if its so motivating I would expect that statement to have more weight."

Zadon gurgled his skin going dusky. "Oh crap." She pulled back again until he could breathe.

Lucian growled, his voice and demeanor going darker. "I have your soulbond you feral waste of space. I rather thought you'd clue into that."

A chill went down her spine. *What soulbond?* "You don't have him. Wanna know how I know?"

Lucian took the two steps to the bars of her cage rattling them. She grinned now confident they didn't have this mysterious him. "Seems like one of us didn't grow up in the last ten years." She pulled her power from Zadon, satisfaction at the thump his body made, distracting her from her own limbs feeling like jelly. "Off you both go to find some nonexistent leverage." She managed a smirk.

She held herself together until they were gone. Collapsing on the rickety bench her emotions dragging her down the forbidden corridors of her mind. Silent sobs wracked her body as she rocked herself waiting for the oblivion of sleep.

Palion was but another prison.

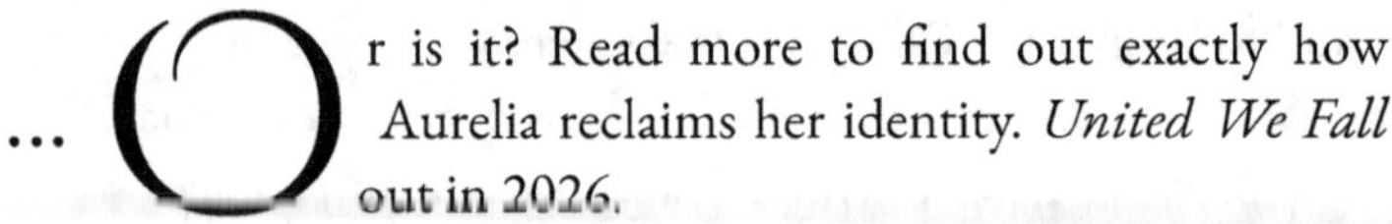

... **O**r is it? Read more to find out exactly how Aurelia reclaims her identity. *United We Fall* out in 2026.

about the author

Mave Hathaway is a writer of fantasy fiction. She contributes to BETA and ARC editing for fellow Indie authors as time allows, eager to aid in supporting fellow authors achieve their dreams of publishing. A prolific writer, she has two different fantasy series in progress, one for adults and one for kids. The biggest hope for her writing is to encourage people to write what matters most to them.

When not writing she is learning how to kick ass in martial arts, teaching young karate hopefuls, and watching movies with her family.

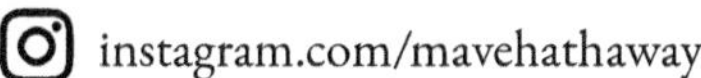 instagram.com/mavehathaway

acknowledgments

The Baelian Empire is a reflection of the emotional turmoil from the darkest days of my life. There are a ton stories yet to tell. I can't believe we are here yet again, a published book ready for others to consume. This was by far the hardest book I have written and I wouldn't have had the strength if not for the following people.

My husband: In the darkest times of our life together he is the one who encouraged me to write adventures. The specific adventures he has requested are still in production but without his belief I don't think I would have picked up the pen. I am beyond grateful to have had you to ramble bits of this book to.

To my chaos gremlin: You won't read this for MANY years. But I hope I do you proud.

My mom: You raised me. You taught me all the ways to survive and without you I simply wouldn't be. I am lucky to have you as my best friend and helper to get this out into the world.

To my sister: You saved Suzu, may you enjoy her new storyline. You are my biggest cheerleader and have been there for every plot hole and twist. I hope you enjoy this.

To my amazing editors; SplitLeafSaturday! You were the first people to read this that aren't included in my family. Though you may as well be my book family. I claim you!

To the newest addition to my team! Keke Davis!! *Insert clapping here* She was the most helpful in the launch of this book and she was a final editor in this manuscript!

To my one faithful Alpha/Beta reader. Your comments made me brave enough to push through this process.

To my ARC readers. Thank you for taking a chance on this Indie Author!!